THE SKY IS DEAD
Sue Brown

Copyright ©2013 Sue Brown

Second edition 2020

Published by One Hat Press

Cover design by Christine Griffin

Formatting by Format4U/Pippa Wood

After being homeless for years, Danny won't survive another winter. Will he accept a fresh start with a new name? Will he take a chance on love? Danny is a typical teenager, his life taken up with friends and school. Then he's caught kissing a boy and thrown out by his parents. He learns fast how to live on the streets, doing what he has to survive, trusting no one.

When he reluctantly rescues a kid being targeted by bullies, he never expects Harry to keep returning. Harry is a force of nature and Danny is swept along. But Danny's luck never lasts and he's homeless and alone once more, determined never to give anyone his faith and heart again.

Living on the streets takes its toll and Danny is faced with a stark choice by his doctors. Will he take that second opportunity of life, a new home, and a new love? Can he take the chance on vibrant Jack, who offers him friendship and more? Is it Danny's turn to look up to the stars?

All Rights Are Reserved. No part of this book may be used or reproduced in any manner whatsoever without written permission, except in the case of brief quotations embodied in critical articles and reviews.

This book is a work of fiction. While reference might be made to actual historical events or existing locations, the names, characters, places and incidents are either the product of the author's imagination or are used fictitiously, and any resemblance to actual persons, living or dead, business establishments, events, or locales is entirely coincidental.

Contents

Prologue

August 2012

"Why do you never mention your parents?"

"Hmmm?" I hadn't been listening, too lost in the feel of Jack's strong hands massaging my feet.

"Your parents. You never talk about them."

I shrug indifferently, not really interested in talking about my family. "They threw me out."

There's a long pause before Jack says, "When?"

"When what?" He digs his clever fingers hard into the ball of my foot, and I hold back a yelp.

"When did they throw you out?"

"Five minutes past twelve on New Year's Day, 2000."

"How old were you?"

"Sixteen."

"Your parents threw you out when you were still at school?"

"Yeah."

He's silent for a minute and then more questions. I know there will be more questions. There are always questions if you are honest.

"Why did they throw you out?"

Reluctantly I open my eyes, because he has stopped digging into my feet and I'm not happy.

"Why do you think?"

"Because you are gay."

"Bingo. On the nose. Ding ding ding for the brainbox."

"But you were a kid." He sounds outraged for me.

"What's that got to do with it? You know it happens all the time."

"I thought that sort of thing didn't happen over here. I thought we were all"—he makes air quotes with his fingers—"enlightened."

I shrug again. "Obviously my parents missed that memo." I wriggle my toes hopefully, but Jack doesn't take the hint.

"What made them throw you out?"

"I just told you that." I try not to snap, but we've been having a chilled evening on the sofa. Him, me, a bottle of wine, and a long, leisurely massage that was hopefully going to end in a happy ending. I was still hopeful that might happen.

No such luck. He tickles my foot enough to make me really yelp. "Tell me why they chucked you out, then."

"Do I have to? It was a long time ago."

"David." I hear the warning in Jack's voice. He isn't going to be deflected, no matter how hard I try. Thirteen years ago I was a different boy, Danny, loved by his parents. Then it all changed.

I sigh and sit up, running my hands through my hair. "I kissed my boyfriend. Dad saw us and threw me out. End of story."

"Your father threw you out of the house for

kissing your boyfriend?"

"That's what I just said. Can we stop with the interrogation now? Do you want a drink? I could make coffee, or we could get another bottle of wine. Do you want more wine? I won't because I've got to get up tomorrow, but I could get you one." I stop babbling long enough to stand up, but he pulls me back down, manhandling me so I'm straddling his lap.

"Please tell me what happened." Jack holds me down with one hand and cups my chin with the other. I get lost in his expression, his eyes dark, the deepest forest green.

"I don't want you to know."

Jack kisses me softly. "I know you don't, but I need to know. Tell me where you lived."

My mouth is dry, and I lick my lips, trying to moisten them enough to speak. It's so hard to talk about this part of my life. All I've ever wanted to do is forget about it. And there's so much at risk telling him the truth. "South London still. About ten miles away from here. It was New Year. We had a party like we always did, and it was the millennium, so everyone was there." The family had been there, as always, even old Auntie Peg and her farting Pekinese. But this time Dad had invited the whole street to see in the new century. "We had the telly on and heard Big Ben." My dad insisted on seeing in the New Year with the chimes of Big Ben, just as he forced us to endure the Queen's speech every Christmas Day.

"Then what?"

"We were hugging and kissing. Everyone was at

it." I'd already been kissed by my parents and all the aunties and uncles, even old Tom down the road had pulled me into a hug so hard I'd had the breath knocked out of me. "Then Steve kissed me."

"Steve was your boyfriend?"

"Yeah. My mum and dad thought he was my best mate. He *was* my best mate, but he was more than that."

"Did you love him?" I hear the jealousy in his voice. I see it in his eyes. This is the first time he's tripped over my past, my ex-lovers. My past is just that—in the past and forgotten. I wish to God I'd remembered that before I'd told him the truth.

"I thought I did at the time. Now, I dunno. We were kids." Of course I'd loved him, with all the innocence and naiveté that a sixteen-year-old possesses.

"So you kissed him in the excitement and your dad saw?"

It hadn't been quite like that. We'd wished each other a happy new century along with everyone else, and then he'd caught my eye, and we sneaked out into the back where it was dark and quiet. He'd pushed me against the wall and kissed me, saying everyone deserved a special kiss. Even at sixteen, Steve had known what to do with his mouth to make me horny.

"Something like that," I agree.

"Then what happened?"

"It was just my luck Dad came out for more beer and caught us kissing. He went ballistic, yelling he didn't want a homo for a son, and then he threw me and Steve out of the house." I can see the pity in his eyes and I hate it, *hate it.* "Don't look at me like that. I'm not a charity case."

He strokes my face with his long fingers, and if I hadn't been so pissed off, I would have purred. "I never said you were."

"You were thinking it, though."

"Maybe a little. What did you do then?"

"We went back to Steve's." I remember the shock I felt as we walked down the street, the numbness in my mind as I tried to get my head around what had just happened.

"At least you had somewhere to go."

I nod. I had—for a while. We'd let ourselves into his empty house—his parents had gone away, which was why he'd been staying with me—and he'd bathed my eye, trying to staunch the blood. In addition to chucking me out, Dad had given me a parting present of a black eye and a split lip.

Unwittingly, he's tracing a tiny scar on my cheek where Dad hit me. "Did you stay there after that or did you have family you could go to?"

I shake my head. "None of them wanted anything to do with me once my dad spread the news. They all told me they didn't want a queer in their house. I stayed with Steve for a bit, but his parents didn't want any trouble. They were having a hard enough time finding out their son was gay."

"So what did you do?"

I look away, not wanting to tell him the truth. Not wanting to admit the shame in my past.

He grips my chin firmly and forces me to look at him. "David, what happened next?"

"I got taken to a halfway home and then I lived rough for a while."

"How long? How long's 'a while'?"

"Over three years."

"Jeez." He lets out a shaky breath, and I can see his eyes glistening in the dim light of the lamp.

That's it. I've had enough. I clamber off his lap and head for the bathroom, giving the pretence of needing a piss. Thankfully he doesn't follow me, and I spend the time staring in the mirror, seeing the frightened little boy I'd been then rather than the man I've become. When I get back he's staring at his hands. He looks up as I come back into the room, and gives me a wan smile.

"Why have you never told me this before? I've known you for over eight years. Why have you never told me about your past?"

"You never asked."

"Don't give me that. You know I did. I've asked you over and over what happened to you, but you never said, and Mary wouldn't tell me."

I smile at that. Mary wouldn't. She's very protective of her kids, even years after they leave her. Really, no one leaves Mary. I've got to know most of her charges, past and present.

He sees my smile and snaps, "It's not funny, David."

My smile fades. "I know it's not funny, but what do you expect me to say?" I hang back by the door, unwilling to face his anger. This was my life, dammit, not his. What the hell right did he have to be angry?

He stares at me. "I met you when you were

twenty. Why did you never tell me about your life? All those times I asked and you'd only just got off the streets?"

"Babe, I wanted to forget that boy ever existed. I still do." That's not me—even if I did just catch a little glimpse of Danny in the mirror.

I can see from his frown he doesn't really understand. Taking a deep breath, I sit down beside him and hold his hand. Maybe now is the time to tell my story. Not all of it, of course. There are things I can never tell him. The things I had to do to eat, to survive. It's a miracle I'm alive and not dead in some alleyway with a needle stuck in my arm. I didn't contract HIV or the clap. I survived, and I can show him that. I'm not a victim and the sky isn't dead.

Chapter 1

I can't remember the last time I thought about leaving my parents' house with only the clothes I was wearing and walking to Steve's place in a total funk. I don't remember much beyond Steve pushing me up the stairs and into the bathroom. I remember him bathing my face with his flannel, washing away the blood from my lip. I catch sight of myself in the mirror. I'm a fucking mess. No one is at home, so Steve holds me for the rest of the night, stroking my head as I cry. I cry for a long time.

The next day he makes me toast and orange squash whilst I ring home. Mum tells me my clothes are outside the garage in bin bags. I put the phone down and stare blankly at Steve.

"What did she say?" he asks as he hands over the plate and glass.

"My stuff is in bin bags outside."

He winces. "Oh fuck, Danny, I'm... that's really fucked."

I sit down and push the plate of toast away from me. If I eat, I'm going to barf. We're still sitting there in silence when Steve's parents come home. His mother takes one look at my face and starts fussing whilst his dad bellows at Steve for an explanation. He looks at me helplessly. I shrug. They are going to find out sooner or later.

His parents receive Steve's stuttering explanation in stunned silence.

"You're both... poofters?" his father asks weakly, latching on to the crux of the issue.

Steve looks at me before nodding.

"My son's a fucking nancy?" Mr Gillan's voice rises, and both Steve and I flinch.

His mother is mouthing, "Oh no, oh no, oh no," over and over.

Mr Gillan slams his fist on the table, making the plates and mugs jump. "You are not queer." He pushes his chair back and storms out of the room.

Steve's mother looks at us with a helpless expression and then runs out of the kitchen after her husband. "Eric, wait," she yells.

"Oh fuck," Steve says. "Fuck!"

When it looks like no one is going to come and find us, we slink back to Steve's room and watch TV. It's nearly two in the afternoon before the door bursts open.

"You can stop whatever you're doing," Mr Gillan starts, but it's obvious that Steve is propped against the headboard watching TV and I'm down at the end of the bed reading a book. Steve's feet had been on my back but he'd moved them hurriedly as the door swung open. Mr Gillan coughs. "Good. Well, I've spoken to your dad, Danny. I'm sorry to say he hasn't changed his mind. You can't go home."

I bite down on my lip to stop the tears spilling over. I'm not going to cry in front of Steve's dad.

"I could call my nan or my aunty."

"You do that," Mr Gillan says.

"Can't he stay here, Dad?" Steve asks.

The answer's obvious before Mr Gillan speaks. "No, he fucking can't. That's not appropriate. We can't have the whole world knowing."

"Knowing what?" Steve says heatedly. "That I'm gay? Is that your problem? The neighbours might find out?"

Mr Gillan shakes his head. "Danny can't stay here. That's all there is to it." He walks out but he leaves the door open.

"What the fuck?" Steve says, but then his mother is walking through the door.

"I collected your things, Danny." She holds up two black bin bags.

I look at the two bags and it suddenly hits me my parents are serious. They really don't want me home. The start of the new millennium and I am homeless. I make a choking sound and Steve ignores his mum to put his arms around me. I'm shaking so violently he has to hold me tight. His mother tuts but we both ignore her.

"Danny—" she starts, but Steve interrupts.

"Later, Mum, okay?"

"We have to talk," she says but leaves the room.

I crumple into Steve's chest, tears coursing down my cheeks.

He holds me, whispering, "It's okay, Danny, you'll be okay. Your nan will have you and your parents will come around."

I accept the words for what they are—blind reassurance. It will be okay. It has to be.

It isn't okay, and it never will be again. But thankfully I don't know that as I cry in Steve's hard embrace.

My nan and my aunt don't want queers in their home. I'm sixteen. My friends all live with their parents. I don't have anyone I can stay with. And Mr and Mrs Gillan make it plain I'm not welcome to stay with them.

Two days after the New Year, we are hiding in Steve's bedroom again when there's a knock at the door and Mrs Gillan walks in with a woman I don't recognise. From the look on Steve's face, he hasn't got a clue either.

"This is Miss Chalmers, from social services," Mrs Gillan says. "She's come to find a place for Danny."

I sit up in a panic. "What?"

Immediately, Steve is holding my hand. "What do you mean?"

"You're taking me into care?"

The woman, a black woman with braided hair, nods. "Kind of. As you're sixteen, we're taking you to a halfway house. You get a room but you get to look after yourself, rather than be looked after." She smiles at me, showing lots of white teeth.

I don't want to leave Steve, but I know I'm not welcome here. Steve's parents have made it very clear they don't want me staying in their house a minute longer than I have to.

"You can't go," Steve says as I stand up. "Mum, tell Danny he can stay."

Mrs Gillan shakes her head. "He can't, son. This is best for everyone."

He glares at her. "Best for Danny or best for you? You just don't want your son's boyfriend in the house. Worried that you might get AIDS from him?"

The worse thing is the horrified look that comes over Mrs Gillan's face, as if that had never occurred to her.

"I don't have AIDS, any more than Steve does. I'm still... we haven't...." I turn away before I embarrass myself any further. I pick up the bin bags sitting in the corner of Steve's bedroom.

"There's some of your clothes downstairs," Mrs Gillan says. "I'll go and get them." She had been kind enough to wash them without complaining.

"I don't believe this shit," Steve mutters, finally letting go of my hand.

I kiss him on the lips, ignoring the social worker. "I'll call, okay?"

"You'd better." Steve sounds all choked up. "I'll see you back at school?"

I make a noncommittal noise, because I don't know what the hell is going to happen to me next.

"You'd better be there," he insists. "I'm not doing that history project by myself."

Steve walks me to the front door and kisses me long and slow, ignoring the noise of disgust from his mother.

I follow Miss Chalmers to her Nissan Micra. She seems friendly enough, but I don't trust her. From the second my father made it clear I wasn't welcome back, I had vowed to myself I would never trust anyone again, especially not a total stranger.

I watch Steve and his mum as we drive away. She has a look of relief on her face but he's distraught, tears pouring down his face. The last thing I see is her putting an arm around Steve and him shrugging it away. I realise sadly that more than one family has been affected by a New Year kiss.

The halfway house is euphemistically called Hope House. I soon learn the kids call it Hopeless House. It is an old house that's been newly decorated. Ten kids are living there, from ages sixteen to nineteen. The theory is the older ones will help us younger ones cook and clean and learn to look after ourselves.

What happens in practice is that the older kids take whatever they like of our things and make us do all the chores. For a few months, as I get over the shock of my parents chucking me out, I deal with living in Hopeless House. I try hard to keep up with my studies at school, and Steve does all he can to help me. Even the school does its best to support me.

I try to fit in, I really do, but I hate living in the home. I miss my bedroom and my home, even Mum's crappy cooking and my small bed. I share a room with Peter, an eighteen-year-old with bad acne and an even worse attitude. The day I get back from school to find my things missing is the beginning of the end of my stay at Hopeless

House.

I don't have much in the first place—my school uniform, some jeans and tops and underwear. Peter is already back from school when I enter our room. I promised Steve I would go round for an hour but I want to get changed first. So far I've managed to keep up with my studies, despite the extra stress. I just want to get through my A levels and then leave school and find a job. I know university is out of the question now.

Peter is on his bed, reading a magazine. He manages a grunt when I say hello. That's about as much as I normally get out of him. I know something is wrong as soon as I look at the couple of drawers I have. They're empty, and the few clothes that were there this morning are gone.

Taking a deep breath to hold back my anger, I grab the edge of the drawer, digging my fingers deep into the wood. "Where's my gear?"

Peter doesn't reply. If the git had nothing to do with it, you'd expect him to deny it or ask what the fuck I was talking about.

"Where is my gear?" I ask again slowly.

When he doesn't reply, I rip the mag out of his hands. He sneers at me. "Where the fuck are my clothes? What did you do with them?"

"I didn't do anything with them, arsehole."

"What did you just call me?"

"Arsehole. Pussy, cunt, buttmunch. That's what you are. You're a fucking queer. Got caught being fucked by your boyfriend and got thrown out for being a homo. Should I be careful about bending over?"

Rage builds inside me. "Yeah. So what? I'm queer. Don't worry, I don't want your saggy arse. Fuck knows what I'd catch from you. Now, where are my clothes?"

Peter curls his lip. "Not gonna tell you a thing, poof."

I leap on him with a scream, hitting him wherever I can reach. He's taller than me and has longer arms, but I'm so angry I don't give a shit. For a minute he's startled, then he tries to hit back, but I'm laying into him for all I'm worth and I'm not going to stop until he's fucking broken.

The noise must have attracted the social worker on duty, because the next thing I know I'm flying back across the room as she tries to separate us.

"What the hell is going on here?" she yells.

Peter holds his nose, and I take satisfaction in seeing it's bleeding heavily. "Don't know. The fucking poofter just went psycho on me."

I'm panting, trying to get my breath back. "He's a fucking thief. He's taken all my clothes. I've got nothing left now."

She looks between the two of us. "Let me get this straight. Your clothes are missing, so you accuse Peter of stealing them?" We both nod. "Then what?"

"He calls me an arsehole and... homophobic names, so I hit him," I spit out.

"Is this true?" She glares at Peter, who shrugs.

"Well, he is a homo."

"Where are Danny's clothes?" she demands.

"How should I know?" It's obvious to me he's

lying, and the social worker can see it too. She shakes her head.

"I'm going to get to the bottom of this if it's the last thing I do. Peter, go and wash your face, and get some ice for your nose. Danny, you don't start hitting before you find out what's going on."

Peter leaves with bad grace, mouthing *homo* at me as he shuts the door.

"He stole my things and called me names," I say stubbornly.

"You don't know he stole your clothes, but he obviously knows where they are."

"He's still a homophobic git," I say.

She huffs out a laugh. "Yeah, he probably is. But you can't hit people just because they call you names. You'll get thrown out of here if you do."

"I don't care."

"You should care. You don't have a lot of options, Danny. You're going to find morons like Peter everywhere. Hitting them isn't going to help your case."

I can see she's serious, but I'm so angry I'm shaking. "What case? My parents threw me out of my home for kissing my boyfriend. This dickhead steals my clothes for being gay. I've got nothing left."

She looks at me with pity in her eyes. "Keep your head down for a while. You'll be fine."

I stare at her and shake my head. "Whatever. I need something to wear." I lie on my bed and roll over so I'm facing the wall. I hear her sigh but I don't pay any attention.

She finds some of my clothes. Peter stops talking to me, as do all the kids in the home. Every time I join them I hear *homo* and *poofter* hissed by the older kids, low enough not to attract the staff. A couple of the younger ones catch me when we're on our own and mutter that they're sorry but they're scared of being the next target. I don't blame them. *I'm* scared of them.

I talk to the social workers to see if they'll move me, but my options are limited. This is a short-term placement, and I'm expected to deal with it. Oh, they make the right noises, but the implication is I have to keep my head down and live with it.

It wouldn't be so bad if the rest of my life—meaning Steve—hadn't gone to shit as well.

We try to keep it going, but it is clear his parents don't want me anywhere near their precious son. Steve starts to make excuses not to see me. At first I believe him when he says it's his parents, but I'm not stupid, and the rumour around school is that he's got a girlfriend. He denies it, of course, and he makes love to me, fucking me behind the garage block until I'm sore and boneless.

Still, Steve is sixteen and he's not that subtle. I see the way Julie Perkins looks at him, and worse, I see the way he looks at her. Now that we're in sixth form, we can come and go when our lessons have finished, and he leaves before me most days.

I'm sitting in Business Studies when I look out of the window to see Steve going through the gate, his arm around Julie Perkins' shoulders. I swallow hard against the lump in my throat at his betrayal. I've lost everything because of him. I have no home, no parents, no family… and no boyfriend. I don't think about what I'm doing, just push back my chair and walk out of the classroom, leaving my backpack behind. Mr Palmer falters, and then calls after me. I ignore him and the buzz of chatter from the other kids. All I can think is this is the end, there is nothing left to live for.

Not sure what to do with myself, I wander the streets until I'm bone cold and decide to head back to Hopeless House. Steve is loitering near the building.

"Danny. Where the fuck have you been?"

I shove my hands in my pockets to stop the urge I have to smack the bastard in the face. "What do you want?"

He hesitates, not looking me in the eyes. "I saw you as I left school."

"So?"

"Julie doesn't mean anything. It's just to keep Mum and Dad off my back."

I grit my teeth so hard my jaw aches. "No?"

He shakes his head. "It's still you and me, kiddo."

"Have you fucked her?" I ask tersely.

Steve hesitates a moment too long.

"Is she a good fuck?"

"No! She's just a cover."

"Poor bitch," I say unsympathetically.

"It's only you, Danny. Just you."

I look into his wide eyes and my heart

crumbles into a million pieces. "Go away, Steve," I say and turn my back on him.

I walk into the home, ignoring his calls, only to be shoved up against the wall, smacking my head against the plaster as a forearm is pushed across my throat.

"What are you doing here, fag?"

I wrinkle my nose at the stench of cigarettes on Peter's breath. "I live here, arsehole."

He presses his arm harder against my throat, against my windpipe. "Not for long. We don't want a bumbandit living here. We'll get AIDS."

"We, meaning you?"

"All of us. So fuck off and live with your queer boyfriend."

I am not going to break down and cry in front of this dickwad. "Can't do that."

Then his eyes light up. "Heard he doesn't want you anymore. Got himself some real pussy, hasn't he?"

There is only one thing in the rush of blood in my head. I punch him as hard as I can, the crack of his nose breaking very satisfying. He steps back with a muffled yell, clutching at his face.

"Danny!" The social worker, Susan, runs down the hallway. "What have you done?"

"He'b a fushing psybo," Peter says, his words indistinct.

She pushes Peter down onto the chair. "Christ, what the hell is it with you two? You can't stay here if you're going to keep fighting, Danny."

I watch her fuss with Peter, and the sick feeling in my stomach intensifies. I walk out the front door, ignoring someone calling my name for the third time that day. Steve isn't there. He hadn't even waited for a minute.

I walk down the street, swallowing hard against the anger and hurt threatening to spill over. I turn a corner and see a sign for the bus station. It's time to get out of this shithole. I've got no idea where I'm going, but no bastard is going to throw me out of my home for a second time. From now on, it's me and only me.

Chapter 2

I roll over, grimacing as something digs me in the back. It's time to replace the cardboard boxes again. They're soggy and I can feel all the stones poking through the cardboard. It doesn't matter how often I clear the soil, stones always seem to creep back during the night to make me feel like a cripple in the morning. I'm eighteen and sometimes I feel like eighty.

I sit up with a groan, peeking out to see what the time is. I don't have a watch or a phone, but I can tell roughly what time it is by the inhabitants of the park. The commuters rushing through to the station aren't there, nor are the kids on their way to school. Aside from a few dog walkers, the park is quiet, which means it's probably before ten. After that it fills up with mums taking their preschool kids to the swings. I roll out from under the thick bush that serves as my shelter and stand up to stretch. I ignore the woman in the smart suit walking past, a disgusted expression on her face. Two years of sleeping rough has knocked the sensitivity out of me. These days that bush is my home. I sleep up against a brick wall that keeps the weather off me and gives me some measure of security. If it upsets the other park users, tough shit. Not that many of them see me at night. They're usually too pissed to see me hiding.

I'm going to head to the drop-in centre at the football club. I can get a cup of tea and a bacon sandwich there that will do until the evening meal at the shelter. I don't bother trying to get a bed, but they let me drop in for a meal. The old guys need the beds more than I do. Sometimes, if I have the money, I treat myself to a burger at lunchtime. I try not to remember the time when I could go to McDonald's every day. I blank out *before*. There is only *now*, and that is enough. Waking up dry is enough of a blessing.

At least I've got rid of the cough now. I caught pneumonia just after Christmas and had to spend three weeks in hospital. It had been the best time I'd had in over eighteen months. Three weeks of being warm and clean and having regular meals. Once I'd cleaned up, the nurses warmed up and took good care of me, feeding me extra food to fatten me up. One of them even brought in some old clothes her kid had grown out of. They were good to me, but I'm not stupid enough to think they would have been the same if I'd been Old Johnny, who's been on the streets longer than I've been alive. Maybe that's unfair; they were good to me.

The social worker at the hospital tried to get me into a shelter afterwards, but places are tight and I didn't want to leave the area. When they start talking about contacting my parents, I quietly left the hospital, despite the fact that my cough wasn't fully gone. It wasn't too cold, and I had new clothes, and I'd nicked a couple of their blankets too. I felt guilty about that, but I figured the NHS saved money on me, so they could afford to lose a few blankets. Going back on the streets was hard, but there is no choice for a kid like me. I refuse to admit I gave them no choice: the only person who makes the decisions for me is me.

I need a wash, but the park attendant is around. I can see him in the distance. The last thing I want is to be caught half naked in the gents by *him*. I don't mind the ones who throw me out, but *him* I don't like. He'd let me have a wash in the gents, but for a price. He should have used the facilities himself, that's all I'm saying. Paying for a wash with a blow job? Do I like having some elderly guy's knob shoved in my mouth? I ignore it like I ignore the cock in my arse for the money for food. They ask for a donation at the shelter for their hot meals, although they don't make a fuss if you can't pay up. I've learned not to be proud, but I help if I can, and sometimes, I don't want the shelter's food. I don't think of myself as a hooker. Shit, I could make more money if I stayed in South London, but I live in a small town not far from Guildford. I don't fancy standing outside Sainsbury's, selling my arse every night to commuters and family men. I do enough to get me a hot meal and no more.

They're pleased enough to see me at the drop-in centre, which is really just a small room in the shelter. Ben, one of the volunteers, looks up from his paperwork and greets me with a cheery good morning as I walk in. I recognise most of the faces now. Old Johnny is already there, in his usual spot. He grunts at me as I walk past. I'll go and talk to him later, after I've had my breakfast. Lil and Billy grin at me from the window seat. In the two years I've been coming to the shelter, I've never seen them apart. Lil's about thirty, I guess, with Billy a few years younger. They're inseparable, despite the fact both of them have learning difficulties. Billy told me the authorities don't approve of their relationship, and each new social worker at the shelter tries to split them up. The last one ended up in Accident & Emergency. Billy took exception to the social worker trying to manhandle Lil and punched the man in the face. The assault earned Billy a few nights in the cells, and Lil went into a decline. It was the intervention of Greg, the manager of the shelter, that got them back together. I think they're the lucky ones, in an odd way. They'd get more help if they were alone, but they love each other and provide comfort and support to each other in the best and worst of times. They don't have to face the bloodsucking loneliness of being on your own twenty-four hours a day.

I'm waiting for my bacon sandwich when Ben appears at my elbow. He's in his thirties and works at the shelter when it suits his shifts as a nurse. He's part of the reason I get treated so well in hospital. Each time I've ended up in A&E, it's been because Ben insisted I go. The first time I resisted, not wanting him to interfere. After that I was too ill to argue.

"Hey, Danny."

"Ben. How's the girlfriend?" It's an old joke. Ben is desperately in love with another nurse. From the conversations we've had, he's been in love with her for nearly fifteen years, but she's never paid him the slightest bit of attention. The first time he told me this, I rolled my eyes and told him to grow a pair. What idiot pines away for that long and never says a word? I am young and naïve. Ben has been homeless. I stared at him in disbelief when he told me that. He nodded at my, "No!" and told me his story. It's depressingly similar to mine. Ben was caught with a boy and thrown out. His parents were in some fundamentalist bullshit church. Gay is a sin blah blah blah. The ironic thing is that Ben is straight. Well, bi-curious, perhaps, but not enough to want to spend the rest of his life with a guy. He's found the love of his life and is never going to do anything about it. The difference between him and me is he accepted the help that was offered and ended up in some sort of scheme for homeless kids. He's always vague about the details. Anyway, he trained as a nurse and spends his spare time working at the shelter. When I ask him why he doesn't ask the girl out, he says, "I'm damaged. What could I offer her?" I have no answer to that. I'm damaged too.

Anyway, any mention of the girlfriend, and he sighs and changes the subject. "I have a suggestion for you."

"No, thanks," I say immediately.

"You don't know what it is yet," he points out.

"Schemes to find me somewhere to live, a job pushing trolleys at the supermarket or wiping the arses of old men."

He glares at me. "No."

I arch my eyebrow and wait.

"Well, okay, maybe. But it's not like the others. This is not an official scheme. It's someone I know who has a bedsit, and it's free at the moment."

"And the catch?" There's always a catch.

"No catch. A few simple rules, that's all."

Yeah, right. "No, thanks, Ben. Why don't you offer it to Old Johnny or Billy and Lil?"

Ben shakes his head. "They don't meet the criteria."

My bacon sandwich turns up. I slather it in red sauce and head for one of the tables. Ben follows me. He at least lets me eat before he renews the attack.

"I'm worried about you, Danny. You can't keep getting ill like this. Your lungs are going to give out if you're not careful."

"I'm eighteen. My lungs are fine." I glare at him, because I don't want to be reminded that whilst chronologically I might be a teenager, sleeping rough is taking its toll. "Chronologically" is a good word. The doctors throw that one at me a lot.

Ben sighs. "This is a good offer, and it might be a couple of years before it's available again."

I finish a mouthful and scowl at him. "You're a good man, Ben, but I won't follow any fucking scheme or obey any fucking rules laid down by someone else. All I want is to look after myself."

He sighs loudly. "Don't fucking swear. For Christ's sake, Danny, don't you want to get a home, maybe go to university?"

"No A levels, remember?"

"You could do an access course. You're bright enough."

I shake my head. I've thought about it, but doing that means I have to trust people not to fuck me over, and I don't trust people. In my own way, I'm happy with my life. I help at the shelter with some of the day-to-day work. They're always short of staff. Ben's taught me how to do basic DIY. I ignore his suggestions that I take a course and learn a trade.

Ben leaves me alone after that, but later on I see him talking to someone on his phone. He keeps looking over at me as he talks, and I have a funny feeling I'm the subject of the conversation.

I help Clare with the dinner preparation, and then Ben wants me to put up blinds in the men's room. It keeps me occupied until midafternoon. I'm tired by then and decide to go for a walk. Not the best timing. The schools are coming out, and I'm faced with the local arseholes who love taking the piss out of the shelter's clients.

You soon learn who to avoid when you live on the streets. People are either hostile to the homeless or they ignore you. Most of them think you're begging for their precious money so you can piss it away on booze. Teenagers are just as bad, if not worse. Usually I roll away under my bush and sleep in the afternoon. They don't know

I'm there.

As I enter the park, I see two dipshits I make a habit of avoiding. I know their names because they yell to each other constantly. Joe is built like a brick shithouse and has the same mental ability, and George is not much smaller. It isn't only me they harass. I've seen them have a go at mums with pushchairs, elderly people, and all the girls that walk past. They are equal-opportunity morons.

They're already pushing some poor kid around when I scurry past. I'm not heading for my bush. I'll go sit in the far corner until they've gone. That's my plan. Until I see Joe twist the kid's arm behind his back. Joe's a sadistic bastard and obviously likes hearing his victim's squeal.

"Leave me alone," the kid shouts.

No chance of that. Joe just laughs and twists his arm even more. "Not going to let go of some ponce," he says.

My steps falter as I go past.

"Homo." As always, George follows Joe's lead.

I look over to see tears rolling down the kid's face. He's deadly white, and I wonder if he's going to faint.

"I'm not a homo," the kid says.

He is. Sorry, kid, but it's obvious even to the blind.

I would have just walked on by, but then George pulls out a knife.

Even Joe is shocked. "Jesus, George, where the fuck did you get that?"

"My stepdad. He said I needed to protect

myself."

Christ, the stepdad is as thick as his stepson.

"What are you going to do with that?" the kid asks, fear written all over his face.

George approaches him with the knife, and then the inevitable happens.

Suddenly Joe lets the kid go, shoving him violently away from him. "Shit! He's just pissed himself."

The kid is wearing dark school trousers, so I can't see, but the smell and the puddle by Joe's feet gives him away.

"Fucking queer cunt," George shouts at the boy.

And that's it. I lose it. Despite the fact the bullies have a knife, I rush forwards, shouting at them to get away from him. They turn to look at me, and I take advantage of their confusion to twist George's wrist to make him drop the knife.

I know if they'd seen me coming I'd never have got away with it. "Fuck!" George yells, and I take great satisfaction in knowing he's in the same pain as the kid must be.

"Leave him alone, you arseholes." I quickly pick up the knife and stand between the kid and the bullies. Of course Joe can't keep his mouth shut.

"Look, the nancy has the bum protecting him. Is he one of your bumboys?"

"Just go," I say, stepping forwards, the knife held rock steady in my hand. It's a miracle, because I'm shaking with fear and adrenaline.

To my relief they leave, but not before spewing more insults. I watch them walk away, making sure they aren't about to turn around and try again. Joe looks over his shoulder and I wave the knife again. He gives me the finger and turns away.

I look down at the kid. To my surprise, the boy is looking up at me with what looks like anger on his face.

"What the fuck did you do that for?" he yells. "I could have handled them."

"You're welcome," I retort.

"They're going to kill me now."

"They were going to kill you before."

"They only wanted to rough me up a bit. It's what they do every day."

I frown at him. "They do this to you every day?" I'd never seen it, but then I'd been avoiding the bullies as well. I feel stupidly guilty that I had been blind to what was happening on my doorstep.

"They wait until I get away from the school and then...."

"And they always threaten you with a knife?"

"That was new. But they wouldn't have hurt me."

I scoff at him disbelievingly. "And that's why you pissed your pants."

"Joe and George... they're just idiots." The kid gets to his feet, pulling a face. I guess the wet trousers are feeling yucky now.

"What's your name?" I ask.

"Harry Cooper."

"I'm Danny."

Harry nods. "I've got to go. Mum's expecting

me home." He picks up his backpack and looks at me.

"'Kay. You see that bush?" I point to where I sleep.

He nods again, a frown on his face.

"I sleep there. You need me, that's where I'll be." I almost laugh at the look of horror on his face.

"You really are homeless? I thought that was Joe pissing about."

"Look at me, kid." I spread my arms out so he can take a good look and watch as he takes in my matted hair, dirty face and clothes.

"I didn't know. Thanks for helping me."

"You're welcome. Bring me a McDonald's next time."

He nods and walks away, squelching a little. He turns once to look over his shoulder. I watch him go and then look at the knife. I can't be caught with something like this. Fortunately the river is nearby and it's really deep at this point. I tuck it under my jacket and walk to the river, then stand on the bridge to look down at the dark water. I've thought about throwing myself off the bridge but I've never had the balls to do it. It's probably not deep enough to kill me anyway, not unless I'm lucky enough to hit my head on a rock. I look around. No one's in sight, so I wipe the handle of the knife and drop it in. It sinks almost immediately. I hope it doesn't get caught by the current and resurface downstream.

In the distance, church bells chime out four o'clock. I might as well head back to the shelter for an early dinner. As I walk, I think of the confrontation with the bullies. I get the feeling I've made enemies today. I swear under my breath, angry at myself for getting involved. I should know better than to get involved, no matter how cute the gay kid. I'm more worried about the fact the kids have knives and seem prepared to use them. Most kids are all gob. Joe's like that. George is more dangerous. He follows Joe's lead, but the fact is, he'd had a knife and seemed prepared to use it.

I can't help looking over my shoulder more often than normal and feel relieved when I reach the shabby white door of the shelter.

Chapter 3

"Danny?"

A hesitant voice disturbs me from my doze. It's warm and I had nothing better to do.

"Danny? Are you there?"

I hear the bush rustling, and tension floods through me. "Yeah?"

"It's Harry. You know, from before. I brought you a Big Mac."

A broad smile spreads across my face. The kid came back, and he brought me lunch.

"Aren't you supposed to be at school?

"It's an inset day."

Inset? Oh yeah, teacher-training day. It's amazing how quickly you forget about things like that.

"How did you get the McDonald's?" The nearest McDonald's is in Guildford, about five miles away.

Color stains Harry's cheeks. "My mum drove me. It's probably cold by now," he says, holding out the familiar brown paper bag.

"I don't care." I can't remember the last time I ate McDonald's. Probably before I left Beckenham. My mouth is actually watering to taste the junk food again.

He's right, the burger's nearly cold, but it doesn't stop me devouring every last mouthful. I am touched at the effort he made. To my surprise, he doesn't leave immediately, instead sitting down next to me on the ground. I feel uncomfortable at this schoolkid sitting so close to me, but he looks just as awkwards. I shift up and wave at the cardboard. "You'll get your arse wet if you sit on the dirt." It rained overnight and the ground is damp.

"Won't be the first time you've seen me with a wet bum," he comments.

I choke on a fry, taken aback by his bluntness.

Harry laughs softly. "Gotcha."

I look at him, chewing thoughtfully. "Tell me why you're here."

He shrugs. "I told my mum what you did to help me."

"Your mum?" I was surprised. I would never have told my ma about something so embarrassing. "What did she say?"

"That I owed you a Big Mac."

"Does she know you're gay?"

"She does now."

"You told her that too?"

"She wanted to know why I'm being bullied. I told her the truth."

"That was brave," I say before I stuff the remaining fries into my mouth. I mean it. After my experience, I wouldn't tell any kid to come out.

"My mum's cool. Her brother's gay, so she doesn't care. She's been dropping hints for a while about me telling her."

"She already knew."

He chuckles again. "Mums always know."

No, they don't, I think, but I'm not going to say anything to scare the kid. He's had a traumatic enough time as it is. "So she drove you to buy a McDonald's for me. How did you know I'd be here?"

"I didn't. Except it's about the same time as the end of school and I took a guess you might follow the same routine."

"I should have offered to share."

He waves that away. "I had mine. Judging by the way you stuffed that down your throat, I should have brought double."

"Next time," I say.

"You think there's going to be a next time?"

"Isn't there?" I counter.

"You don't seem bothered that I'm... gay." Harry stumbles over the word, and I get the feeling he's not said it out loud too many times.

"You don't seem bothered I'm homeless."

He looks disappointed at my reply. I know what he was fishing for, but he doesn't need to know about me. He doesn't need to know that not all mums are so accepting of their son's sexuality.

"How old are you?" he asks suddenly.

"Eighteen."

He looks shocked. "Is that all? You look older."

"Thanks," I say drily.

"Um, I didn't mean—"

"I know what you mean. I look like shit."

"Yeah," he says promptly and then flushes even

harder. "Oh fuck, I've said it again. I don't mean that."

"How do I look, then?" I ask, arching an eyebrow.

"Like someone who didn't have the luck I did."

His blunt honesty takes me by surprise again, and I have to swallow really hard against the lump in my throat.

"Yeah, well, my parents weren't so happy to find out their son was a homo."

He stares at me with wide eyes. "What did you do?"

"Do? I did nothing. They threw me out."

"But why?"

"I just told you."

"Because you were gay?"

"Yep."

"But—"

"Listen, kid, I don't want to talk about it, okay?"

He looks offended. "I'm not a kid. I'm only two years younger than you, and I'm taking my GCSEs."

Sixteen? Jesus, he looks about twelve.

"Oh yeah? What did you take?" I wasn't that interested, but if it kept him from asking questions about me, that would be cool.

"Geography, German, French, and Sociology."

"I took History, Business Studies, Music, and Drama." I laugh at his surprised expression. "What? You think I'm too stupid to take my exams?"

"What? No! What did you get?"

"As, Bs, and Cs. Enough to start my A levels."

"Is that when you got thrown out?"

I nod. "What are you going to do about the morons that were having a go at you?"

Harry shrugs. "Nothing I can do, except avoid them. I think you scared them, because they went in the opposite direction the last couple of days."

"You be careful of George," I say.

"You mean Joe."

"No, I mean George. Joe is just a loudmouth, but George had the knife and he was going to use it on you."

"I always thought of him as a cling-on, like Goyle and Crabbe."

I stare at him blankly. "What?"

"You know. Malfoy's hangers-on."

"Who's Malfoy?"

He gives me that wide-eyed, bemused expression again. "Harry Potter?"

"Harry Potter is a Klingon?"

"No, he's not a Klingon! Harry Potter is a wizard!" Harry bursts out, clearly exasperated. "Don't you know anything?"

I raise my eyebrow. "Obviously not."

He catches the edge in my voice and blushes. "God, sorry. I forgot. You've probably not read *Harry Potter*, have you?"

"No. Heard of it, but I didn't read much. More into sport than books."

Harry nodded. "I hate sport. Well, football. That, and rugby. My school believes contact sport makes a man. I can't wait until I'm in the sixth form and don't have to do PE ever again." He shudders. "I hate school. Can't wait to finish and get away to uni."

A pang shoots through me and I have to look away, not wanting him to see how envious I am. Then he touches my arm. I jump, not used to someone touching me voluntarily.

"I'm sorry," he says.

I press my lips together, nodding to show I accept his apology.

"I've got to go soon. My mum wants to go to my gran's for tea."

I'm disappointed, but it was fun while it lasted. "Thanks for the burger."

"No worries. Thanks for your help with those morons."

"You be careful around them, okay? Don't let them get you on your own. I'll look out for you here." As soon as the words are out of my mouth, I regret them. His eyes light up, and I know he's looking forwards to seeing me—*me*—again. Now I have a commitment to protecting the kid. Jesus, why couldn't I have kept my mouth shut?

"I'll be careful," he promises, and he awkwardly backs out of the bush. I don't follow him. There are too many people about. I settle back down to sleep away the afternoon until it's time to go to the shelter. My belly is full of burger and fries, and for some stupid reason, I feel happy. Fucking pathetic.

I don't get why Harry keeps coming back after school. He misses odd days when he sees other friends, but he's always there the next day. George and Joe stop hassling Harry in the park once they see me watching, although he admits that out of my sight, they aren't always so pleasant. I promise to be more visible, although I'm wary of going too near the school. Kids are shits to bums like me.

Harry does more than just bother me every afternoon. Most days he brings food. Not McDonald's, but the local burgers or southern fried chicken. I tell him to stop spending money on me, but he doesn't take any notice. It's all junk food, and I notice I'm putting on weight.

The day he brings a new jumper and a pair of gloves, I protest.

Harry dumps the usual bag of food next to me, together with another carrier bag.

I scowl as I poke the carrier bag. "What's this?"

He flops down beside me. "Just something I spotted in a charity shop."

"You've been looking in charity shops?" I ask skeptically, opening the bag reluctantly to find a blue V-neck jumper and a pair of gray gloves. "I don't need these."

He waves his hand, saying, "Winter is coming, and you'll need all the clothes you can get."

I give him a cool look. "It's June. Summertime."

"And the temperature really dropped last night." The little shit won't back down.

Unfortunately he's right. It's warm during the day, but last night was chilly.

"I can't store anything extra. I haven't got a rucksack."

I shouldn't have been surprised when he brings a rucksack along with the food the next day. I hold up the label from TK Maxx, still attached to the bag.

He flushes. "It's an old one my granny bought me."

"Yeah, right. Don't treat me like I'm stupid, Harry."

Harry shifts around to face me. "I don't think you're stupid at all. But I want to give you stuff I don't need."

"Not if you're buying them for me," I say stubbornly.

His bottom lip wobbles, and then he glares at me just as stubbornly. "You need them."

"No, I don't."

"Yes, you do!"

"I don't need your charity." I push the bag away and get to my feet.

Harry looks up at me. "What *do* you need, Danny?"

"Nothing. I don't need you, I don't need you to buy things for me, and I don't need you to feed me. I managed without you so far. I don't need you," I repeat. I nearly cave at the hurt in his eyes, but it has to be said. "Take the rucksack and I'll get you the clothes. Don't come back."

Harry jumps to his feet. "What are you so fucking scared of?"

"I'm not scared."

"Yeah?" He folds his arms. "Keep telling yourself that. One day you might convince yourself." For a kid who was pissing in his pants a few weeks ago, he's right in my face.

"Fuck off, Harry. I'm not in the mood to play

your games."

"I'm going. Keep the bag. You can stick it over your head and ignore the rest of the world."

He walks off again. I'm getting sick of watching him walk away. Stupid kid.

"Harry, don't. I'm sorry." For some stupid reason I can't just let him go.

Fucking idiot keeps walking, dodging around a mum with a double pushchair and a scruffy black dog. Taken by surprise, the dog bares its teeth at Harry. I push between Harry and the dog, worried the dog is going to take a snap at Harry.

"Watch it!" The mother glares at us both, and then looks at me a little more closely. I see the expression of disgust and fear cross her face. Perhaps she thinks I'm going to mug her, or kidnap her children.

I notice the moment Harry clocks her expression. Anger crosses his face and he opens his mouth to say something. I don't give him the chance, hauling him off to the side and out of her way with a muttered apology. She looks at us again. We must look incongruous; the nerdy clean kid and the bum. I steer him away from her and towards my bush.

"What the fuck?" Harry tries to pull away from me but I've got a firm grip around his bicep.

"I don't need anyone paying attention to me," I say. "The fewer people who see me, the better."

"Perhaps you ought to stay under the bush, then, instead of out in the open," he says snarkily.

"You can be invisible in a crowd," I point out.

He drops his gaze. "Yeah, I know." Harry has

spent his entire school years trying to be invisible. I feel sorry for him. I had Steve. We didn't give a shit who saw us. I was luckier than Harry, in a way.

"I'm sorry for being a dick," I say.

He nods. "Sorry for walking off like that. It was either that or punch you. I was worried you'd hit back."

I raise an eyebrow. "Have you ever hit anyone?" I ask.

Harry shakes his head. "No. Instinctive reaction, I guess. Too much time being around morons like Joe and George."

"Yeah. We had them at my school."

"I'm sorry if I made you feel like a charity case. I didn't mean to." He looks at me earnestly, and those green eyes... my stomach flip-flops as I stare into his eyes. I haven't felt like that since forever. Since Steve. It makes him even more dangerous, and I want to run away and never be found again.

He's breaking down the barriers I've carefully erected against the world since leaving Hopeless House. I am screwed.

Chapter 4

To give myself something else to think about, I hang about at the shelter, talking to Lil and Billy. I notice Lil's looking thin and drawn, and Billy is sitting real close to her. I bring over three mugs of hot chocolate and sit with them after dinner. Lil looks tired, and Billy draws her in for a hug. Even though it's stupid, envy coils in my gut at their obvious closeness.

Since Steve's betrayal, I've never wanted to get close to anyone. There has been a growing anger in me at the way I lost everything and Steve lost nothing. My parents cared so little about me they threw me out for one kiss. Steve cared so little he got a girlfriend even before I was out of the picture. I know he was sixteen, but so was I, and I loved him and needed him. I watch Lil and Billy, and hurt just a little more.

When I take the mugs back to the counter, Greg looks over at the couple and I follow his gaze. Billy is stroking her face and she's leaning into the caress.

"I think the doc ought to look at Lil," I say. "She's been a bit pale lately."

Greg shakes his head. "He already has."

"What is it? Anaemia?" It's a common problem

for the homeless, with our poor diet.

"You know I can't tell you that."

No, he can't, but between the sadness in his face and the way Billy is acting, I get the feeling Lil's got more wrong with her than a simple blood disorder.

"Is it serious?" I ask.

"It's up to Lil to tell you, but, yeah, it's serious."

It's more than serious, but I don't find that out until later.

I wander back to the park just before seven. Harry is already waiting for me under my bush. It makes me laugh how at home he's made himself, wrapped up in one of the hospital blankets.

"Hi." I flop down beside him with a grateful sigh.

"Hi."

Before I can breathe, Harry rolls me onto my back and straddles my thighs.

"Wow, you happy to see me?" I ask, grinning up at him.

"Always," he says and bends down to brush my lips.

I wrap my arms around him to kiss properly, but Harry squeaks, and I let him go.

"What's wrong?" I ask.

"Something's digging into my ribs." He pats my pocket.

"Oh!" I pull out the toothbrush and toothpaste. "I wanted to be prepared," I say, embarrassed.

He grins at me. "How sweet."

I try and push him off, aware my cheeks are burning, but he doesn't let me go. "You *are* sweet," he says.

"Girls are sweet. I'm not a girl," I growl.

He deliberately rolls on my groin. "Yeah, got that." The little fucker is going to have me creaming my joggers.

"Thought you wanted a kiss."

He thrusts against me again. "I want to do more than kiss."

I catch hold of his hands, which are fumbling at my waistband. "Wait."

Harry frowns, but he does stop. "What now?"

"You're sixteen. I'm not going to... to...."

"Fuck me? You don't want to fuck me?" He tries to get off me, but I'm still holding his hands. "Let go of me."

"No. Stop struggling. I just want to talk to you."

"You don't want me. You just said so."

I close my eyes in exasperation. "Harry, you're sixteen...."

"And boys my age fuck. We've already had this conversation."

"They *talk* about fucking—a lot."

"You were with Steve."

"Steve and me, we'd been friends for years."

He looks at me uncertainly. "You're telling me I have to wait for years before you'll fuck me?"

I shake my head. "No."

"Then...."

"I get fucked to earn money," I say, more harshly than I intended, because I feel him flinch.

"You're a hooker?" He tugs on his hands and this time I let him go. He rolls off me and brings his knees to his chest, wrapping his arms around them defensively.

This isn't the way I intended the evening to go. I sit up and shuffle over to him, then pull him into a hug. "I'm not a hooker, but, yeah, sometimes I need money and this is the way I earn it."

"Can't you get a proper job?" Harry sniffles, and I realise he's trying hard not to cry. *Way to go to stamp on a kid's dreams of a first time, Danny.*

"No, not like most people. I need somewhere to live. An address."

He looks up, his eyes glistening with unshed tears. "Don't you want a home like everyone else?"

"We've had this discussion," I remind him gently.

"But...."

"But nothing. To get a home I need to get into a scheme, and to do that I need to give up my independence. And I'm not going to do that. Not now. Not ever."

"You're not sixteen anymore," he says. "It's different now."

"Now I'm eighteen I'm treated as an adult, but it's all about the schemes. They can't put me in the system, but it's still doing what they want rather than what I want."

He sniffles again. "Wouldn't that be better than letting some old perv stick his knob in you for a tenner?"

"I charge more than that," I say, offended.

"I'd pay you to fuck me," Harry says. "I could pay you instead and then you wouldn't have to get fucked by people you didn't like."

I'm so shocked, and horrified, I let him go. "I'm

not going to charge you to fuck me."

"Why not? You let other men."

"You're not other men. I lo... care about you!" I stumble over my words, but fortunately he doesn't seem to notice.

"I don't see the difference."

I pull him close again. "There is a huge difference between what I let them do to me, and what I want to show you. You deserve someone like you. Not a... slut like me."

"Fuck, I don't understand." He drags me in for a kiss.

I know Harry doesn't understand and that's part of the problem. He's too young to appreciate that I can separate what I do to survive from what *I* want to do. I give up and let him kiss me. The playfulness and teasing has vanished and now it's just clumsy desperation. His teeth graze my lip painfully as he presses even closer. I let him control the kiss for a moment, and then I take over, gentling the kiss, coaxing him to softer movements. It seems to work. Harry relaxes his hands, which have been clutching my back, and his mouth slackens under mine.

When we pull back for air, he grabs me by the hair and holds my head in place almost painfully. "Don't you dare fuck anyone else while you're with me." He's fierce, demanding that I give him what he wants.

I close my hands around his wrists. "I can't make those sorts of promises," I say gently. "I will always keep you safe. That promise I can make."

"By not fucking me?" he asks bitterly.

"By taking things slowly and always using a rubber."

"You promise you will fuck me soon."

I nod. Soon is a moveable target. He just doesn't need to know that.

Chapter 5

Lil is sick. It doesn't take a doctor to work that out. She spends most of her days lying on the cushions in the bay window, her faithful shadow stroking her hand. Billy tells me she has breast cancer, which has spread to her brain and her bones. Inoperable and so advanced there is little point trying any treatment. "All they can do is make her comfortable," he says. Lil smiles at him when he says that. She's fine as long as he's there by her side.

I see the way the doctor tries to manage her pain. It seems to get worse every day, and the doctor makes gentle suggestions that she should be moved to a hospice for respite care "until the pain eases." Lil is adamant that she wants to stay with Billy at the shelter. Billy just wants whatever Lil wants. I know at some point Greg is going to have to insist Lil be admitted to the hospital or the hospice. The shelter isn't organized for intensive nursing. Greg is trying to arrange for Billy to stay with Lil until the end, but both of them are fighting any idea of transferring her to the hospital. I think they know she won't come back.

Midway through November, I come into the shelter to find the window seat empty. I'm not surprised. Lil has barely been conscious the last couple of days.

Ben catches my gaze. "She's gone to the hospice."

I nod. Billy had finally agreed Greg and Ben could make the arrangements to get Lil transferred to the hospice, with Billy, when the time came. "Does she need anything?" I ask.

Ben shakes his head. "She won't last the night."

"What about Billy? Will he come back here?"

"I doubt it."

I did too. Billy's whole life had been tied up with Lil. He wouldn't want to come back to the place where they had been happy together.

The next day, Harry comes to find me. I'm still wrapped up in my blankets and the sleeping bag he provided. I haven't moved all day, not even to go to breakfast.

"Hey."

"Hey."

Harry doesn't bother talking. He takes off his coat and crawls under my blankets and wraps himself around me. It's drizzling, but with the brick wall and the thick canopy of evergreen leaves as protection, it isn't too bad in my shelter.

I lean back against him, snuggle as close as I can. I haven't cried—at all—even though the news came that Lil had died around 5:00 p.m. But being in Harry's arms loosens the knot of grief inside me, and for a few minutes I weep for the loss of a friend. Harry doesn't say anything. He holds me close and kisses me occasionally. When the tears finally end, he waits for a while and then hands me a wrapped package. A cheese and pickle sandwich. Despite my continuing efforts to get him to stop, Harry keeps feeding me. He has stopped feeding me junk food every day. The sandwich is his idea of healthy food. The flask of chicken soup is even more welcome.

"Lil?" Harry asks eventually. He knew the end was close.

"Yeah. Yesterday afternoon." I use the flask cup to warm my hands.

"I'm sorry, Danny." Harry strokes my arm. It's too close to the way Billy caressed Lil, and I almost pull away.

"Me too."

"What's happened to Billy?"

"I don't know. By the time I left, we'd only just got the news."

"You can find out when you go for a meal."

I turn away. "I don't think I'll go today."

"Why not?"

"Just don't feel like it. It would seem odd without her."

"I think everyone will be feeling the same," Harry says.

"Yeah." I can't deal with everyone. I just want to sleep and forget the world exists for a while.

Harry says nothing more for a while. The rain gets heavier and seeps through the canopy of leaves. He looks up as raindrops run down his face. "It's going to rain all night."

"Yeah?" I don't pay much attention to the

weather. I'm either wet, or cold, or both.

"Wait here." Harry suddenly disappears. I wonder where he thinks I'm going to go. I pour the last of the soup, realising I'm still hungry. I'm getting used to three meals a day. I'm getting soft.

I've no idea how long he's gone, but by the time Harry comes back, I've bedded down for the evening with as many layers over me as I can to shelter from the weather.

"Come on," he says.

I frown. "Where to?"

"My house. Mum says you can come round for the evening to warm up and she'll cook us both dinner."

My heart sinks at his excitement. "No, thanks."

Harry frowns, his excitement dimming. "Why not?"

"I don't need looking after. Lil died. So what? I just need to sleep."

"Are you being a twat again? Yeah, I want to see you out of the rain for a few hours. If you won't go to the shelter, then come home with me. You can get cold and miserable later. At least have something to eat."

"I'm fine here," I say stubbornly.

"And you'll be even better at my house."

"I said I'm fine." My voice rises in anger.

Harry scowls at me. "You're coming home with me. Mum knows about you. She knows you're homeless, and, yeah, she's worried about my friendship with you, but she also knows you saved me from Joe and George."

"She won't want me in her house, then." I latch

on to the one part of the conversation that makes sense.

"Fucking hell, why are you such a stubborn git? Get off your butt now."

I try to out-glare him but I'm not winning this battle, and before I know it, I'm being dragged along to Harry's home.

It's a semidetached on one of the streets near the park. His home is bigger than the one I grew up in, but not so much it makes me feel inadequate. No, what makes me feel totally inadequate is the look Harry's mum gives me when we walk in the door. I'm used to distaste from the general public, but Mrs Cooper has an additional worry—that I'm corrupting her son.

Harry doesn't seem to notice. "Mum, this is Danny. Danny, this is my mum."

"Pleased to meet you, Mrs Cooper," I say awkwardly as I drip on her doormat.

"Danny," she says, and then she seems to look at me a little closer. "How old are you, Danny?"

Harry leaps in before I can speak. "Eighteen. I told you that already."

I frown at Harry. "Nearly nineteen." Only just over a month to go to another birthday I won't celebrate.

"Just a baby," she mutters. At least I think that's what she says. "Harry, take Danny upstairs and show him where the bathroom is. I bet you could do with a hot shower. You can lend him some of your clothes. I'll put dinner on for you both."

I open my mouth to protest but then shut it again. To her I probably look disgustingly filthy, although Harry would know how much effort I've made to keep clean since we've been kissing.

Harry whoops for some reason and grabs hold of my hand. His mum looks at our joined hands and I wait for her to lose it, but for some reason her face softens, and she smiles at me. I follow him up the stairs and then into the bathroom.

"Here's a towel, and if you give me your clothes, I'll get them washed for you." He leans forwards and turns on the shower. "It's nothing special, but you should be able to warm up. I'll go in after you because I'm cold as well."

Harry stands looking at me expectantly. I raise an eyebrow. "Are you waiting for me to get undressed?"

He flushes immediately. "I... sorry... I didn't think. I... just throw the clothes outside the door." He backs out.

I snicker quietly. I would have stripped if he'd made an issue of it. The shower is amazing, and there's no one yelling at me to stop wasting the hot water. I take advantage of the shower gel and shampoo, although nothing can get rid of the tangles in my hair. I don't linger too long although I could have stayed in there for an hour.

When I open the bathroom door, unsure what I'm supposed to wear, there's a pile of clothes just outside. There's also a Harry, who is sitting, waiting for me. "You could have stayed in longer," he says as he hands me the clothes.

"That's okay," I say. Suddenly I feel exposed. I'm wrapped in a towel, but Harry is staring at me hungrily, his gaze trailing over my body. Even with the extra food Harry's been feeding me, I'm still very thin.

"Harry, does Danny like broccoli?"

His mother's shout breaks the eye contact between us, which I'm really grateful for, because another minute and Harry and I will be breaking all the rules.

He looks at me inquiringly. I shrug, not sure why she didn't ask me herself. I'll eat broccoli if I have to.

"Yeah!" he yells.

Before we go back to the eye-fucking, he points me in the direction of his bedroom. "Get dressed while I have a shower."

His bedroom is large and covered in books. The boy has more books in his bedroom than I've read in my entire life. I get dressed quickly, sure I'm going to look ridiculous. I'm shocked to discover the joggers fit me. I realise in the few months I've known Harry, he's grown at least four inches. He's almost my height. I just hadn't noticed.

I drape the damp towel over his desk chair, and then sit down on Harry's bed to wait for him. It's an odd feeling. Harry is the age I was when I was kicked out, and his bedroom could have been mine... except for the books. Again, the loss I try to keep buried deep kicks me in the gut. I look through the stack of textbooks on his desk. This should have been me.

Harry comes in with a big smile on his face. "That's better. Fuck, I was cold."

My mouth drops open when he strips off his

towel and reaches for his clothes. He's not as confident as he's trying to appear, and his hands shake. Harry is lean, rather than skinny like me, without much body hair. I make sure he sees me checking him out—fully—figuring that's what he wants. He's gorgeous and I make sure he knows it. Harry blushes, but I can see the pleasure in his face as he gets dressed.

"Boys! Dinner!"

We both jump at his mother's yell, and Harry throws on a hoodie as quickly as he can. I laugh outright when he gets his arms tangled up and has to struggle to pull it down. He growls at me and I laugh again.

His mum lets us sit in front of the TV to eat our dinner. Harry makes me watch *Hollyoaks*, which I hate, but I'd have watched anything just to relax in front of the TV again. It's going to be hard to go back out into the cold night again. Perhaps Harry's mum has some more cardboard I could use.

When we're finished eating, Harry curls up in my arms to finish the episode. Mrs Cooper raises her eyebrows at the way we're sitting, but she doesn't comment. Harry has no idea how lucky he is.

As she takes the plates away, Mrs Cooper says, "I'm going out. I'll be back by eleven. You won't be here, Danny, okay?"

"Yes, ma'am," I say promptly, and she nods approvingly.

Harry looks like he's going to protest, but he shuts up when I elbow him in the ribs. When she's gone—off to see some friend or other—he turns to me.

"Well?"

Confused, I frown. "Well, what?"

"We're here—alone—and it's warm and dry."

Oh. My mouth goes dry. "Do you think we should? What happens if your mum comes back?"

"She's out for the evening. She won't be back." Harry straddles my lap and looks at me expectantly. "Danny, do you want to fuck me or not?"

I grip his thighs. "I'm not going to fuck you, but I'd like to blow you."

He shudders. "Yeah," he says hoarsely, and he clambers off my lap. "Where do you want me?"

"Have you got a rubber?"

"Yes, but, I haven't... you know...."

I press a kiss into his stomach. "I know, but I haven't been checked out. I might even have something like a mouth infection. I'm not risking your health."

"We're going to get you tested," Harry insists as he leaves the room.

He's back in seconds with a condom and lube. "How...?"

I hold out my hand. "Come here."

I undo his fly and push down his jeans and boxers. Harry is hard, his cock slapping against his stomach. His prick is thick, the tip glistening already. Fuck, I'd like to take him in my mouth and swallow him whole, but I promised to keep him safe. I rip open the condom packet, and Harry moans as I smooth the rubber down his cock. He clutches my hair painfully.

I look up. "You can hold on, but I'm not going bald, okay?" He moans again as I jack him for emphasis. Perhaps I should have spoken first.

I hold his arse with one hand as I wank his cock firmly with the other. I want his first experience to be amazing, to blow his mind. I want him to compare every other blow job he gets to this one for the rest of his life. I want to be remembered for *something* other than being a street kid. I suck in the head, ignoring the taste of the latex. He tightens his hands on my head but doesn't pull my hair out.

I tease the slit first, and then lick all the way around the head until Harry's moaning so loud, I pray his neighbours are out. Thank God we didn't try this in the park. When I feel Harry's thigh muscles tremble, I sink down on his cock, clenching my throat muscles around the head. His soft pubes tickle my nose. That's just a taster for what's to come. I pull back to lick and explore the shaft, until he's begging me to deep-throat him again. I thank God for all the experience the nameless men have given me as I let him fuck my mouth. His shaft swells in my mouth, and he yells as he comes, filling the condom with his hot jizz.

Harry's legs wobble and I pull him forwards onto my lap. He sinks down against me, resting his head in the crook of my neck. I stroke the back of his neck as his breathing calms.

Eventually Harry raises his head. "Fuck," he manages.

"Not today."

He shoves my shoulder and looks down at his

limp cock, still covered by the rubber. "Ugh, I think I need to get rid of this."

"Don't get rid of your cock. I like it." I pat it gently.

"Haha!" Harry says sourly, heading for the downstairs loo.

I hear it flush and then he comes back.

"Danny?"

I open my eyes. I hadn't even realised I'd closed them. "Huh?"

"What about you?" he asks, kneeling at my feet.

"I'm fine."

"I want to do the same to you." He tugs on my tracksuit bottoms. I raise my hips and he pulls them down. It's hard for me not to laugh at the look on his face—horny and petrified at the same time.

"Take your time," I say, relaxing against the cushions. I hand him a condom. Harry looks as if he's about to protest, but it's nonnegotiable. Harry's hands shake as he fumbles rolling the condom down my dick. I wonder if he's tried to put one on himself before now.

He pulls a face at the taste of the latex, but he goes back for another try, sucking in my cock as far as he can. He gags and flushes, his cheeks burning, but I stroke his hair.

"Use your hands as well."

He's a fast learner, and I don't take long to come, spilling out into the condom in quick pulses. Harry looks triumphant at his success.

After we clean up and get dressed again, Harry gets two cans of Sprite to wash away the foul taste in our mouths. It'll be time for me to leave soon. I'm trying not to think about it, but I know once I'm wrapped up in my blankets I'll be okay. I can't get afford to get soft or I'll never survive the winter.

Harry snuggles in my arms again, watching the end of some drama. I don't pay much attention and doze off towards the end. I wake to a beeping sound, and Harry wriggling forwards to get his phone.

"It's a text from Mum." A look of glee crosses his face. To my surprise, he holds it out for me to read.

Rain is worse. Danny stays in spare room. 1 night only.

I bite my lip. "Are you sure you want me to stay?"

Harry rolls his eyes. "Don't be fucking stupid. Course I'm sure. I don't have to be at school 'til ten, so we can sleep in and get some breakfast."

We spend the rest of the evening on Harry's bed, exploring each other's bodies. I make him come again, a slow hand job that has him whimpering and curling his toes. We're in separate beds by the time Harry's mum comes back—just.

He kisses me good night once I'm in the little bed in the spare room and goes back to his own, getting into bed just before his mum opens the front door. It takes me a while to fall asleep. I listen to the rain falling against the window and thank the God I don't believe in that I'm not out there tonight. I hope Billy is warm and dry, wherever he is, and wish Lil a safe journey, free from pain.

Chapter 6

I walk Harry to school the next morning before I make my way to the shelter. Greg looks up as I arrive, a relieved look on his face.

"Danny, I was worried when you didn't show yesterday."

"I'm sorry. I needed some time to deal."

Greg nods. "I know. You weren't the only one. Glad you're okay, though."

I look over my shoulder to the window seat, unreasonably angry when I see Liam, one of the old-timers, sitting there. "Any sign of Billy?"

"No, and I don't expect him to come back, at least not for a while."

I look at the window seat again, feeling a pang of loss. "Have you called the police?"

"Waste of time," he says sadly. "He'll come back if he wants to." He gives me a tight smile, and I wonder how many Billys have come and gone over the years.

I look at the seat one last time and make my peace with it. Lil's gone, Billy's gone—life moves on.

Greg hands me a cup of hot chocolate and says, "Someone called yesterday evening, asking for you."

"For me?" Who the fuck would be looking for me?

"They wouldn't leave a name. It was a woman."

My first thought is my mum is finally looking for me, but then I realise how stupid that sounds. My parents would have no clue where I am now.

"What did you say?"

"Nothing. I asked them to leave a message, and they put the phone down."

"Bizarre. I wonder if it was Harry's mum, checking up on me."

"Harry's mum?" Greg raises his eyebrow.

"Uh... someone I know." I will my rising blush away. I fail. It isn't helped by the glee on Greg's face.

"Have you got a boyfriend, Danny?"

"No."

"No?" He sounds disbelieving.

"Maybe," I mutter.

"Good for you."

I expect more questions, but he just ruffles my hair and goes back to his paperwork. I'm not sure whether I'm disappointed or not. It would be nice to have someone interested in what I'm doing.

I spend the day at the centre. It's raining and my bed is saturated; I checked it this morning. I'm going to need to check the bins behind the shops for more packing cases. I could do with another sleeping bag, as well. Harry made me bring my old one to his house to dry it out, but his mother took one look at it and dumped it.

I doze in the armchair by the radiator until it's time to meet to Harry. The rain's stopped and

Harry's really happy when we meet. Makes my day brighter. Sunshine and a fucking gorgeous boyfriend. I keep wanting to touch him, unable to believe he's all mine. He grins when he sees me and pulls me behind a tree to kiss me. We're both grinning at each other when we pull apart. I've got another problem as well, not helped by Harry's hand brushing it.

I grab at his wrist. "Don't do that or I've lost my only clean clothes."

He looks disappointed, but then a mischievous grin spreads across his face. "Mum is out 'til seven. Want to come and watch TV? Make out for a while? You can take a shower if you want. I could scrub your back," he adds helpfully.

"Are you sure your mum won't mind?"

He nods and for a moment the smile slides off his face. "She offered. There's dinner there for you as well. If you want, you can stay the night."

I bite my lip. "I can't do that, Harry."

"Why not? It's going to rain again tonight."

"Because it's taking advantage of her, and that's not right." I hesitate and he notices.

"What? Why won't you accept her help? It's only a bed and a few meals."

"What happens if I get used to being looked after, and then you don't want to see me anymore? Then I'm back as I was before, only this time with no nice food and no soft bed. I need to be independent, Harry. You've been great and all, but I'm getting soft."

"Bollocks!" he says, and he drags me through the park.

"It's not bollocks."

"If the hostel was offering the same thing, a couple of nights' free food and a bed, would you take that?"

"Well, yeah. But that's different."

"No, it's not. The weather is crap and you have the chance to sleep in a bed. Take it and shut up."

I protest again, but Harry ignores me. He does that a lot, I've noticed, when he doesn't get his way.

He makes me strip when we get home and hands me what I wore yesterday, already washed and dried. "Go in the shower. Don't rush. There's plenty of hot water." I open my mouth to protest, and he places one finger across my lips. "Shut up, Danny. Just get clean."

I stand under the shower for a long, long time, letting the warmth seep through until I'm wrinkled. When I get out, Harry has heated up the dinner, and we sit and watch kids' programmes. Harry starts fidgeting next to me after a while. I look at him to discover the reason for his fidgets. I bite back a grin. "Want me to do something about it?"

He's caught the zip of his jeans in his boxers. It's at half-mast and there's nothing he can do about it. Harry's glowing bright red, but he nods, placing his hands by his side. He hisses when I slide one hand in and graze his dick with my knuckles.

"Careful!"

"I'll be careful. Don't want this to get hurt." I deliberately stroke his cock, feeling it twitch under my fingers.

"Bastard!"

"Do you want me to free you up or not?"

"Only if you suck me off."

I raise an eyebrow. "Giving me orders now, are you?"

"You have your hand over my dick. I'll do anything you want."

I snicker as I gently free the cotton of his boxers from the zip. Okay, so maybe I'm touching him a bit more than I should. By the time I finish, his cock is leaking and hard against the back of my hand.

As soon as the zip is free, he raises his hips and pushes his jeans and boxers down. "Fucking suck it!" he orders, grasping his cock with one hand and pushing it towards my lips.

"Wait, condom."

He looks around frantically, as if he expects one to miraculously appear. "They're in my bedroom."

"I'll go and get one."

"In the bedside table. Hurry."

I run up the stairs and into his bedroom. Fortunately, they're where he said, and I'm back downstairs and rolling one down his dick in a couple of minutes. He's virtually shoving his cock into my hands, trying to jack himself off. I can try to control matters or I can just let him do what he wants. Within seconds he's at the point of coming. I rip off the condom and let him spurt over my hands.

"Oh fuck. Oh fuck. Fuck!" he yells.

"Didn't realise you were going to be a screamer."

"Shut up," he grumbles.

I am prepared as he looks around. "Here." I offer him the box of tissues I took from his bedroom.

He cleans himself up and looks at me. "Er, sorry?"

I grin at him. "For what?"

"Coming so quickly. Jesus. I thought I was going to burst. Kind of messed up the big ending."

"Hmm, you did, didn't you."

Harry looks mortified, but I just laugh at him and lean forwards to give him a kiss. "You're so hot."

He stares at me uncertainly. "I am?"

I stroke his soft belly. "Yeah. You're really hot, and I want to do that again."

"Fuck me," he begs, but I shake my head.

"Not yet."

"Why not?"

"Because it's a really big deal, and when we do it, it's got to be right."

"I don't see why it's that big a deal," he says.

Sighing, I get off my knees to sit next to him on the sofa. "I know you don't, but believe me when I tell you it is."

He stares at me uncertainly. "Was it a big deal for you?"

"Yeah. But I loved him, so it was all right." I can see the jealousy in his eyes. "It was a long time ago."

"You're only eighteen," he points out.

"It was a lifetime ago." My time with Steve feels like a world away from where I am now. I was naïve, happy, selfish, and self-centreed, like all sixteen-year-old kids. Now I'm tired and worn out, but I know what's important, and I'm going to make sure Harry does as well.

He doesn't look convinced, but tough. He'll deal with it.

A noise outside attracts my attention. "Is that your mum?"

Harry snaps his head up. "Shit, she's home early. Shit shit shit!" He tucks himself away while I dispose of the condom.

When I come back down the stairs, Harry is talking to his mother. She smiles at me as I walk into the lounge.

"Danny, hi."

"Hi, Mrs Cooper. Thank you for letting me come back and for the dinner."

"No need to thank me after all you've done for Harry. He told me about that awful boy with the knife and how you saved him."

"He's done more for me since then."

It's true. Since we met, Harry has fed me and given me clothes, but more than that, he treats me like a human being, rather than some garbage to be ignored on the street.

"Harry told me what happened to you. I can't believe your parents threw you out because you're gay."

I give her a tight smile. No matter how hard I try, I will never get over that moment of betrayal. I think she sees how upset I am because she mutters something about getting changed and leaves us alone.

Harry wraps his arms around me and I rest my head on his shoulder. We stay like that until I hear her coming down the stairs again.

I raise my head and smile at him. "I ought to go."

He frowns at me. "We've had this discussion. You're staying here tonight. Look, it's raining now. Don't be stupid, Danny."

Mrs Cooper glances between us as she comes in. "Is there a problem?"

"Danny thinks a couple of nights in a bed will make him soft." Harry's holding on to my wrist as if I'm about to burst out of the door.

She nods as if she understands. How can she understand?

"It's bad out there again, Danny. Sleep here one more night, please?"

I sink down onto the couch. "One more," I say stubbornly, "and that's all."

"Good." She nods. Then she says to Harry, "You need to do your homework, young man."

Harry looks mutinous but she stares him down.

I touch Harry's arm. "Do your homework and I'll read or watch TV."

"You can play on the PlayStation if you want," Harry suggests, but I see the look on Mrs Cooper's face.

"Another time," I say.

He nods and gets out his schoolbooks. I start watching some crappy drama, but I doze off before the end. I only wake up when I feel a kiss on my cheek. "Come on, you. Let's go to bed."

I yawn as I sit up. The clock tells me I've been asleep for over an hour and it's nearly nine o'clock. "I'm sorry," I say to Harry's mum. She is sitting in the corner reading the *Daily Mail*. "I didn't mean to fall asleep."

"She dozed off too," Harry crows.

Mrs Cooper scowls at her son. "You can shut your mouth. I didn't fall asleep. I just shut my eyes for a minute."

"More like half an hour."

He grins at his mother's glare. It's nice and normal, and makes me feel relaxed being with them.

Harry leads me upstairs after we both say good night. Outside the bathroom door, he hands me a blue toothbrush.

I take it and look at him curiously. "What's this for?"

"It's a toothbrush."

"No shit, Sherlock. Why are you giving it to me?"

"So you can keep one here, and not worry that you've got bad breath. No excuses!"

I bite my lip. My toothbrush is in my pocket. I wasn't going to leave it where someone could nick it. When I've used the bathroom, I find him waiting for me in the guest bedroom... in the bed... in his pyjamas.

I shut the door hurriedly. "Harry... your mum... she'll kill us... me!"

"Not if we're quick. You missed out, remember?" He gives me a filthy, wicked grin.

My cock doesn't know whether to hide or point straight to Harry. I'm eighteen. It makes up its own mind.

"Fuck." That's all I can manage as I lie down next to him in the small bed.

"I wish." Harry kisses me, soft and gentle, as we lay together in the bed. He reaches up to stroke my cheek, and I try not to flinch. It's hard to explain I find it hard to be touched, even by Harry. Since I left home, the only people who have touched me have been nurses or johns.

Not knowing what is passing through my mind, Harry slips his hand into my borrowed boxers and cradles my cock. I push forwards into his grasp.

"Do it," I whisper. "Just do it."

He does, hesitantly at first and then with more confidence, fisting my shaft until my toes are curling and I'm reaching for more. Harry pulls me forwards with his free hand, and I bury my head in his neck as he strokes me harder. He pulls my climax from me until I'm sobbing quietly into his shoulder, and then he strokes me through each pulse. A sixteen-year-old kid reduces me to this, a messy, quivering wreck in his arms.

He cleans me up and then climbs back into bed and snuggles up against me until I wrap my arms around him.

"I thought you were going to your own bed," I say, happy to have him there, warm and comforting, but worried about his mum suddenly appearing.

"I asked her not to come up for an hour."

"You did what?"

"Asked her not to come upstairs for an hour 'cause I wanted to say good night to you properly."

"And she agreed?" I squeak in amazement.

Harry nods against my chest, the strands of his long hair tickling me. "My mum's awesome, huh?"

She's more than awesome. "Why is she so cool about me? You've brought home a boy, and more than that, a homeless kid, and you've told your mum you're having sex."

Harry doesn't answer immediately. I start to worry and then he says quietly, "I told her that you'd refused to have sex with me straight away."

"Oh?" I wasn't sure what to say.

"She knows you stopped me from getting stabbed or worse, that although you're homeless you don't take drugs or drink. You were polite to her and didn't expect to be invited back. She knows you take care of me by not rushing things and by being careful. Christ, Danny, some of the skanky mares at school screw around without any protection, and the boys just use them. I've chased one boy and he takes care of me by saying no."

"Why is she so cool about you being gay?"

"Her brother was gay. He died of AIDS complications about ten years ago. When she found out about me, she was scared for me, and then you come along and look after me. You walk on water as far as she's concerned."

I process this for a moment. "I envy you so much." The words get caught in my throat.

Harry shifts so now it's me wrapped in his arms. "I hate your mum and dad," he whispers, "but if they hadn't hurt you, I'd never have met you."

That's true. I think of how my life would have been, and wonder if, just maybe, I'm a little lucky after all.

Chapter 7

I don't really need to visit the drop-in centre for breakfast, but because Harry's at school and the weather isn't great, I have nowhere else to hang out. Ben is behind the counter when I walk in, pouring tea into a mug for Old Johnnie.

Johnnie takes his mug and retreats to the window seat, grunting a greeting when he sees me.

I smile and make my way over to Ben to say hello. He doesn't return my greeting, and when I look closely I can see he's been crying. "Ben? Are you okay?"

He sniffs loudly. "We got some news about Billy."

I have a sick feeling in my stomach. "What's happened to him?"

"They found him near the railway line this morning."

"He got hit by a train?"

Ben shakes his head. "The transport police think he was more likely electrocuted by the rails. Billy was drunk. One of the police dealing with the case recognised him as one of ours."

I blink back the tears. I liked Billy. He'd been a friend from the time I arrived in town. It was he who showed me where to find cardboard to pad out the beds and where to find thrown-out food we could eat when we had no money.

"Hey, drink this and sit down. You look like you're going to pass out, kid."

Normally I'd have glared at him for calling me kid, but I'm still in shock. Ben hands me a hot chocolate and I take it over to the chair by the radiator.

I can't believe he's gone, but I'm not surprised. Billy was only a few years older than me. He'd always been happy, but once Lil died, so did his happiness. I sip the chocolate, making it last. I'm short of money now. I've not *earned* any since my relationship with Harry got more intense. I'm going to have to separate out our lives if I'm going to keep eating. I can't rely on Harry to feed me. He does feed me, every day. But what happens if one day he doesn't? Then I'm like Billy. Screwed. Billy was a good man and now he's gone because he was too dependent on Lil.

I'm deep in thought and don't see Ben sit down in the chair next to me.

"Greg tells me you've got a boyfriend."

I shake my head. "No, not a boyfriend."

Ben looks confused. "So you're not seeing a guy?"

"I am, I was, but not now. Not after what's happened to Billy."

"What's Billy got to do with you and this other boy? What's his name?"

"Harry," I say absently.

"So what's Billy's accident got to do with you and Harry?"

I look over to him. "Don't you see? Billy got dependent on Lil, and now they're both gone. What happens if I get dependent on Harry and then he leaves? He's been feeding me and bringing me clothes. I've spent two nights at his house. What happens when that all goes wrong and I'm left with nothing?"

Ben looks startled. "I didn't realise you were that involved with him. It's not the same, though. Lil and Billy both had learning difficulties. They were both homeless. If we'd been sensible, we'd never have allowed them to get so close. Harry lives at home. How old is he?"

"Sixteen."

"He's a kid?" Ben makes it sound as if I've been molesting a child.

"I'm eighteen," I remind him. I draw up my legs to my chest and hug myself defensively.

He sighs. "I know. It's just... you are nothing like a normal eighteen-year-old."

"Thanks for reminding me I'm not normal. What gave it away? Is it that I'm queer?"

"You know that's not what I mean."

"What do you mean, then?" I'm not going to make it easy for him, even if I am thinking the same things he is.

"Does Harry know about you?"

I stare at Ben incredulously. "Of course he does. How the hell can I hide it? I can't take him home to Mummy."

He studies me carefully. "You've changed over the past few weeks. Apart from your hair, you don't look like a bum. You're clean and you've put on weight."

"That's because he's been feeding me and I'm wearing his clothes. He knows where I sleep. We've been friends for months, and no, I haven't fucked him, and yes, we've used condoms to blow each other. Satisfied?"

Ben nods. He doesn't look embarrassed at my answers. I guess it takes more than a snarky answer about sex to embarrass a nurse. "And you've slept at his house?"

"Yeah, and I've met his mum."

Suddenly he breaks into a large smile. "That's great, Danny."

I look down into my mug. "Yeah, I guess."

"You don't think it's great?"

"Of course I do, but it's going to go wrong and I'm gonna be the one that's hurt, aren't I? He gets to keep his nice house and his mum, and I go back to sleeping in the park." I stare into my mug to avoid looking at Ben.

"What makes you think it's going to go wrong?" Ben sounds confused.

"He's sixteen. You don't stay in love with the same person when you're sixteen. Steve dumped me and he was sixteen. Harry'll do the same."

"You know that for a fact?"

I look at him, exasperated. "Kids don't stay in love," I repeat.

"Some do." Ben's words are so sure I look up. He gives me that regretful look.

I roll my eyes. "*You* have never done anything about it." The unrequited love for that nurse is hardly the same thing.

Ben sighs. "I know, and I wish it were different."

"Go and talk to her. Christ, you'll be dead before you say anything."

"It's not that easy."

My eyes are getting exercise today. "Ben, you're a nurse. You have your own home. You volunteer at a homeless shelter. What more could a woman want? Stop making excuses."

"Like you're doing?" he snaps back.

"Ha fucking ha!"

"Billy and Lil loved each other."

"And look what happened to them!"

Ben sniffs and I almost feel guilty... almost. "All I'm saying is, don't give up on love," he says. "If Harry's not the one, then there'll be someone. But you've got to get off the streets. Trust me. That's the first step."

I shake my head. "If I was going to trust anyone, it would be you and Greg, but trust is stupid."

He stands and holds his hand out for my mug. "Do you want to end up like Old Johnnie or Liam?"

"I'm not like them. I don't drink or take drugs."

"So? Neither do they. They've been homeless for so long we can't help them more than we do. I thought you were different. I thought we had a chance with you."

Ben walks off before I have a chance to reply. I scowl at his back. He doesn't know me. He doesn't know how scared I am. Billy's death has proved to me that becoming dependent on someone is a bad idea. I told Ben to commit to the nurse, but he's got the right idea. Trust no one.

I sit in the same seat until it's dark, long past the time I should meet Harry. Eventually the drop-in shelter closes for the day, and I wander back to my bush. There's a note tucked in a sleeping bag—a new sleeping bag.

Waited for ages. Come to the house.

I wrap myself up in the sleeping bag, ignoring how hypocritical it is to use the bag, and try to sleep. I miss the warmth and softness of the bed in the guest room. I miss my Harry.

I spend a fitful night asleep only to wake up and find Harry sitting next to me. Harry missed me the day before. Harry is furious when he discovers I avoided him deliberately, particularly the reason why. Harry doesn't hesitate to tell me what he thinks of my stuttering explanation.

He sits on the sleeping bag, his face pinched and his eyes blazing at me. "So you spent all day avoiding me because I might split up with you?"

"It's not that simple." Almost Ben's words. I'm glad the nurse is not here to hear me.

"Jesus fucking Christ, Danny, what do I have to do to prove I love you?"

I stare at him, wide-eyed and speechless.

He stares back, pressing his lips into a thin line.

"You love me?" He *loves* me?

"I may be sixteen, but, yeah, I love you. I haven't spent the past few weeks feeding you because I'm still grateful. And, yeah, it may not last, but so what? Mum and I'll make sure you're okay. You won't get thrown out with nothing again."

"You're too young to know what you're talking about."

"You're only two years older than me," he snaps. "Did you love Steve?"

"I thought I did."

"Well, I know I love you. And you're not going to give me that trust bullshit again."

"I'm scared."

Harry's expression softens. "I know. Look, I've got to go to school. I'm already late. I'll meet you back here and we'll go home, okay?" He leans forwards to kiss me, and I can taste the cereal he had for breakfast on his lips.

He backs out of the bush before I have a chance to reply. *Bastard.*

I'm back, waiting for him, by three o'clock. I've showered and cleaned my teeth at the shelter, and put on the cleanest of my few clothes. I have a change at Harry's. It's cold, so I wrap up in the sleeping bag and wait for Harry to arrive.

When he hasn't arrived by four o'clock, I'm worried. By five, I'm frozen and pissed off. I decide to walk to his house to see if I was mistaken and he meant me to meet him there. When I get to Harry's house, I can see it's in darkness, so I sit down on the front doorstep to wait for him or his mum. Neither of them turns up, and by seven, I can hear the church bell chime out the hour, and

I'm too cold to stay any longer. I've missed dinner and I'm going to go to bed hungry again. Harry didn't bring any food this morning.

Harry doesn't turn up the next day, either, or the day after. I've been back to his house every couple of hours, but no one is there. One time I see a neighbour staring at me from a window, and I leave hurriedly in case they call the police.

I go to his school and hang around for the day, hoping to catch a glimpse of him, but nothing. I see Joe and George. I hang back, hoping they don't see me. I want to ask someone, but who the hell could I ask?

On the third day, three men dressed in black suits come out of the house. They look serious, and I know whatever's happened to Harry and his mum, it's not good.

"It's so sad, isn't it?"

I jump as someone speaks behind me. I look over my shoulder to see an old lady staring over at the strangers in Harry's driveway.

"They were good people. I'm going to miss Mel and Harry." She clucks her tongue sadly, and then shuffles down her garden path without waiting for me to respond.

Tears roll down my cheeks as I realise I've lost my boy, and my happiness, and my life.

I also have a more pressing issue. I'm really hungry and I have two choices: I can beg for the day or earn some money to get some food. I've gone soft from being fed every day.

As I enter the park in the afternoon, I see the park ranger making his rounds in the van. He spots me and nods towards the toilets. I nod and pray it won't take long.

As soon as the gents door is locked, he pushes me to my knees and undoes his fly.

"Not seen you for a while. Ahhh."

I shut him up as I slide the rubber he gives me down his cock with my mouth. It doesn't take much to suck him to full hardness, and I close my eyes as I blow him, trying to imagine that the skinny dick in my mouth is really Harry's. The grunts and sighs he makes keep intruding on my fantasy.

Eventually—not soon enough—it's over and he comes with a noisy shudder. I wait as he tucks himself away, and then he hands over a twenty.

He unlocks the door and leaves, a satisfied expression on his face. He's barely out of the door before I lurch into a stall, my stomach heaving as I puke on an empty stomach. I feel like I've cheated on my Harry. Not my Harry. Not anymore.

I wash out my mouth, spitting into the basin to try and get rid of the taste of vomit. I leave the toilets, intending to head to the local shops to get some food. Instead I walk to the shelter, the desire to see a friendly face greater than anything else. It's getting dark now, and the occasional streetlight casts a faint glow along the path that leads to the shelter. I'm lost in my own thoughts, and the footsteps behind me take me completely by surprise. I don't have time to turn before something slams into me from behind and knocks the air out of me. I try to take a breath, but my lungs don't seem to cooperate. Footsteps running away make me look up, and I think I see Joe and George legging it away from me, although my eyesight's woozy.

My legs give out and I sink to the ground, facedown in the dirt. I don't know what's happened to me.

I can't breathe. Someone is sitting on my back and squeezing the breath out of me. I want to tell them to get off. I turn my head to see Ben leaning over me, his eyes wide, and he's talking. I know he's speaking, because his mouth is moving, but I can't hear what he's saying.

I can't breathe. Perhaps I'm having a heart attack? It'd be a relief. There's nothing I want to stay here for anymore. Now Harry's gone. Harry's left me. Steve didn't want me, and Mum and Dad threw me out. What is the fucking point of staying?

I try to look up but I can't see anything except blackness. All the stars have gone out. I think the sky is dead.

Chapter 8

October 2003

I stare up at the ceiling, feeling I've just been given a death sentence and the sound of the doctor's footsteps are leading me to the grave, rather than just moving to the next patient. Well, that's it, then. I am officially fucked.

Go out on the streets again and die.

No placebo (go me, I remember the word), no "*you have a risk of getting pneumonia*" or "*you need to take more care of yourself.*"

This time the Grim Reaper told me one more bout of pneumonia would kill me. My lungs are fucked over from all the infections, and since the stabbing last year, I'm even more vulnerable. The year has taken its toll on me, and the doctors have told me bluntly that reaching two decades is looking increasingly unlikely. My twentieth birthday is in just over two months.

There's no point telling the registrar the second they throw me out, I'll be back under my bush in the park. They talk to me about shelters and work schemes, yadda yadda, and I try not to yawn.

Might as well accept the inevitable. I'm well enough to be discharged now and there's no point delaying until it's really fucking cold. It would only be harder to adjust again. I sit up and look in my locker. My clothes are there in a green hospital bag. I dig them out. Filthy dirty, blood-stained, and torn. I shudder as the memory floods back of rough hands pulling the joggers off me, nails tearing the skin of my thighs, and the thought of putting them on again makes me feel physically sick.

"You're not wearing those again."

I look up to see one of the nurses in the gap between the curtains. "I haven't got a choice, Sylvia."

"And that's where you're wrong, young man." Sylvia produces a small pile of clothes.

"Young man? You can't be more than a couple of years older than me."

Yeah, yeah, I am sucking up to her—the woman is old, forty at least—but she is nice, unlike some of the other bitches who've made it plain I've been taking up space.

Sylvia snorts and laughs loudly. "Flattery will get you everywhere." She hands over the clothes—black joggers, a gray T-shirt, and a black hoodie. "I guessed the sizes. We can change them if needs be."

I frown as I look at the pile. They aren't left over from other patients. These are new clothes, with the tags still on. "Did you buy these?"

She nods. "I did."

"I can't accept them, Sylvia. You shouldn't be spending your money on me." But when I try to hand them back, she takes a step back.

"Get dressed, Danny. I want to have a talk, and it's not easy when your arse is flapping out of the gown."

Immediately, I look over my shoulder. Of course my bum isn't exposed at all. I was sitting down, for fuck's sake.

"Gotcha!" she crows.

I flip her off halfheartedly. "I'm gonna get you." It's a feeble threat and it's reflected in her face.

But she sobers up and points at the clothes. "They aren't expensive. I just got them at the supermarket. You need them, Danny. You can't wear those rags. They should have been binned."

I swallow hard against the lump in my throat. "Thanks."

Sylvia looks at me knowingly. "Get dressed and we'll talk."

"Aren't you on duty?" And then it strikes me she isn't in her usual dark-blue scrubs.

"Not today. There's someone I want you to meet. We'll go grab a coffee at the café."

I open my mouth to ask more questions, but she flaps her hands at me and disappears into the ward. Shoving my soiled gear back into the bag, I look at the clothes. She's tucked boxer briefs and socks into the joggers. My cheeks heat at the thought of her buying me underwear. I pull off all the labels and get dressed. She's got my size almost perfectly, the length just a little too long.

Shoes! Where are my trainers? I get off the bed to hunt in the locker, but I can't see any sign of them. I push back the curtains.

Sylvia is chatting to one of the other nurses a little way down the ward. She looks up as I emerge and smiles. "Ready to go?"

I point at my feet "Where are my trainers?"

"Damn, I didn't think about shoes." She frowns and looks at the other nurse. "I don't remember you wearing any. Your feet were bare when you came in."

Lighted cigarettes pressed into the soles of my feet. Yeah, those guys didn't just sexually assault me. They liked torture as well.

The other nurse, a quiet young blonde with bad skin, clicks her fingers. "There's a couple of pairs of trainers in the linen cupboard. What size are you?"

Size? I struggle to think. I don't bother with actual sizes now. "Nine, maybe."

She rushes off and comes back a moment later with a pair of well-worn black Nikes. They're too big, but beggars can't be choosers, as my gran used to say, and I'm definitely a beggar.

"Come on, then," Sylvia says. "Mum'll be wondering where we've got to."

"Mum?" I wasn't expecting to talk to anyone else.

"Yes, my mum wants to meet you. She's been nagging me for the past week, but I wanted you to have a clear head before you met her. Mum's...." She laughs softly, and I feel a pang of jealousy and loss. "Mum is a force of nature."

I shake my head, not sure what she means.

"You'll see."

I can't force any more information out of her,

so I shut up and follow Sylvia to the café. As we walk in the door, a woman sitting at one of the tables gets to her feet. The resemblance is immediately obvious. Sylvia's mum is a smaller, more wrinkled version of her daughter.

"At last. I thought you'd forgotten about me," she grumbles as Sylvia kisses her on the cheek.

"Like I could do that," Sylvia says, and I can hear the exasperation in her voice.

I stand back, shifting uneasily from foot to foot. I don't know why Sylvia wants me to meet her mum, and it's making me nervous. The urge to run is strong.

"So this is the young man you haven't stopped talking about?"

Sylvia's mum fixes her gaze on me, and I have to resist the temptation to salute.

"Here he is. Danny, meet my mum, Mary Wilson." She tugs me forwards to meet her mother.

"Pleased to meet you, Mrs Wilson." I'm not entirely sure that's true, but I make the effort.

She nods. "Polite. Nice to see you've got manners, Danny."

I resist the urge to make a snarky remark and remain silent.

"Are you always this quiet?"

"Not sure what I'm supposed to say, ma'am."

Mrs Wilson nods again. "Well, sit down. Sylvia can get us drinks whilst we talk."

"Cup of tea, Danny, or a Coke?" Sylvia asks.

I look over at the selection. "May I have a Tango?" I haven't had a choice in a long time.

"Sure thing. Cuppa, Mum?"

"And some biscuits. Get Danny whatever he wants. You must be hungry if you've had hospital food for weeks."

"I know what Danny likes. Be back in a moment." Sylvia wanders off to the counter.

I resist the urge to rush after her and look at Mrs Wilson.

She waves at a chair. "Sit down, Danny. You must be wondering what this is all about."

"Yeah."

"Yes, not yeah."

"Yes, Mrs Wilson," I parrot obediently.

"Better."

"Sylvia tells me you've had a rough time."

"Yeah. Yes." I nod, because *rough* is one way of describing it. Not the word I'd use.

She looks at me with an expression I don't recognise. I'm used to seeing pity, disgust, and rejection. Mary Wilson looks interested in me, and I don't know why.

"Why were you on the streets, Danny?"

"If you know what happened to me, you probably know my parents threw me out." I go on the offensive, and I'm not surprised when she nods.

"Why did they throw you out?"

"What does it matter?"

"Did you steal from your parents, or hurt someone? Were you in trouble with the police? Take drugs?"

"No!" I say hotly, temper rising. The old bitch has no right to suggest such things.

"Then why did they throw you out?"

"Because I'm gay. My dad caught me kissing my boyfriend and threw me out."

Mrs Wilson nods again, and I can tell from the look on her face she already knew that.

"Sylvia told you, so why ask me?"

"Because Mum likes to know a boy is honest before she offers him a home," Sylvia says as she puts a tray on the table.

"Wh-what?" I stutter the word in shock.

Mrs Wilson rolls her eyes. "For heaven's sake, Sylvia, what did I say about taking this slowly? You're going to scare the poor boy away before I've even spoken to him."

"Danny's not a kid anymore." Sylvia looks at me. "My mum has a bedsit in her house that she offers to young people like you."

"Like me?" I say stupidly.

"Kids—sorry—who've had a rough time and need a break. It's a short-term thing, so don't go thinking it's a permanent home. But she offers you somewhere to live rent-free until you get a job and can find more permanent accommodation. You don't believe me?"

My lips twisted in a sneer. "Rent-free? I'm gay, ladies. I don't service women."

If I expect them to be shocked, I'm sadly mistaken. "You won't *service* anyone under my roof," Mrs Wilson says firmly. "It's your place, with your own front door and key. My only rules are no drugs and no prostitution. If you want to bring a boyfriend back, that's a different matter."

"But why me?"

Sylvia lays her hand on mine. I resist the urge to pull away from the kind touch. "Danny, you're one step away from killing yourself. Winter is coming, and you won't survive out on the streets. The doctors told you that this morning."

"I can find a shelter," I say stubbornly.

"But you won't. You never have. Danny, think about this. You've been very ill. You've had to recover from the assault and pneumonia and bronchitis. We didn't think you were going to make it at one point. And last year you got stabbed. You nearly died then. All we're asking is you give yourself time to have a fresh start."

I look at Mrs Wilson, who has been letting Sylvia do the talking. "What do you get out of it?" No one ever, *ever*, gives something for nothing.

She doesn't answer and instead digs her purse out of her bag.

"I don't want your money, lady."

"I'm not giving you money. I'm offering you a home."

She opens the small, leather wallet and shows me a picture. I recognise her and Sylvia, although Sylvia looks to be around my age. I don't recognise the boy.

"This was my son, Allan."

I pick up on the past tense. "Was?"

She nods, her eyes fixed on my face. "He was seventeen when he died. He was attacked outside a pub near where we lived. A gay pub. The first time I found out my son was gay was when the policeman told me he was dead, killed by a group of drunks who decided to pick on the skinny kid coming out of the pub."

I look at the picture. I know what Mrs Wilson is saying: it could so easily have been me. Nearly was me a few weeks ago. It should have been me. Allan had been loved by his family. I was just some loser on the streets.

"Soon after Allan died, I met Sharon. Her mum kicked her out for being trans. She stayed with us for six months, until she got a job. I promised myself no other gay child would die if I could do something about it. I can't save them all, just one at a time."

"Why not foster a teenager? Someone younger, who needs a home. There are plenty of them."

Mrs Wilson touches the image of her son with one fingertip. "My son was gay. I look after gay children."

I need space to think. To give myself time I pick up the forgotten fizzy drink and take a long swallow. Around me the world carries on, oblivious to my turmoil.

Sylvia is giving me a sympathetic look that makes me want to grit my teeth. "I know it's a lot to take in. We've done this at least twelve times now, and we know what you are feeling. Would it help to talk to one of Mum's kids?"

"I can do that?" For some reason that startles me.

"We keep in touch with most of them."

"Most? Not all?"

"Some can't stick to the rules," Mrs Wilson says as she puts away her wallet. "I don't have many, but I expect those I do to be kept. Just as you would if you lived at home."

I bite my lip, but I know she's right. Mum and Dad would have expected me to abide by their rules.

"What about rent? I've got no money."

"You can sign on and claim for housing benefit. Mum will show you how to do that." Sylvia puts down her cup of tea and gives me a frank look. "We're not trying to take over your life. I know you're independent, and you've survived this far, but another bout of pneumonia—hell, even cold or flu—and you're not going to make it. This way you get a roof over your head and a chance to recover for the winter. Danny, you're not well yet."

The inside of my mouth is getting raw from all the biting. I know I'm still fucked up. I can feel every breath, and just the short walk to the cafeteria has done me in. Still, the thought of being dependent in someone else's house.... I know how to get money if I need it, and it doesn't involve begging. Being on my knees, yes, but that's my choice.

"Tell you what, Danny...."

I look up to see Mrs Wilson giving me a shrewd look. "Yeah?"

"*Yes*. It has an *s* on the end. Stay until you feel well enough to move back to the streets."

"You won't force me to stay?"

She rolls her eyes at me. "I'm not into kidnapping young men."

"Mum prefers older men," Sylvia confides.

It's on the tip of my tongue to make some

crack about wheelchairs, but she's not my mum.

"I do not," Mrs Wilson says hotly.

"John Carpenter? Mick Lawson?"

"They were friends, that's all."

"Uh-huh."

Mrs Wilson splutters. She's all flustered, and I can't hold back the grin when Sylvia shares a slow wink with me.

"Don't you give Danny any ideas. He's moving into a good house."

"I'm only teasing you, Mum. He can see you're a good person." Sylvia looks to me for confirmation.

I nod immediately because I can see that, and I'm rewarded by both the women beaming at me. Fuck knows why she wants to take random guys into her home in memory of her dead son, but I can see she means well.

Mrs Wilson gets to her feet. "Sylvia's going to walk you through what happens if you decide to stay. I have to go now. I've got a date at the community centre."

I stand up too and hold out my hand. "Nice to meet you, Mrs Wilson."

"Mary," she says as she shakes my hand.

"Huh?"

"Call me Mary, and don't say 'huh'. It makes you sound stupid."

I look over to Sylvia to be rescued, but she shrugs. "Get used to it, Danny. She's a menace when it comes to the English language."

"Just because I insist it should be spoken correctly does not make me a menace," Mary says primly.

"Just don't call her a Nazi," Sylvia says in a stage whisper.

"I'm going to ignore that. Give me a kiss and I'll see you later, Sylvia." Mary leans forwards.

Sylvia bends to give her mother a kiss. "See you later, Mum. I'll bring in dinner."

"What do you like to eat?" Mary asks me suddenly.

I'm thrown. "Anything I can get," I admit honestly.

"But before. What did you like eating when you were at home?"

"A roast dinner or lasagna. I loved Mum's Sunday roast."

"Roast lamb it is, then," Sylvia says. "Me and Mum love a roast."

"It's not Sunday," I say, outraged. "You have roast on a Sunday."

Mary looks at me with a serious expression on her face. "We'll make an exception, just this once. I'll cook, Syl; you just bring the boy."

I realise I'm being stupid. I rarely get the luxury of a roast dinner and I'm arguing about what day of the week it is? And then I realise they're already assuming I'm coming to their house.

"Does anybody ever turn you down?" I ask sourly.

Sylvia grins at me. "Not after the bribe of a roast dinner."

Despite the resentment at their casual assumption, something inside me just *folds*. It's the first time in years I haven't had to think for myself—since Harry, anyway—and it's like a blockage has cleared and I can breathe. I want to say no, I can survive on my own, thanks, but I can't. Even if I accept the dinner and not the bed, they aren't asking for my mouth or my ass. Okay, it's some sort of therapy for the old lady. *Mary, not the old lady.* But if it benefits me for a while, then fuck it.

I suddenly realise they haven't said anything, and I look up to see them smiling at me. I sigh and rub between my brows. "I don't do the washing up."

Mary snorts. "Good Lord, that's what a dishwasher is for. You can clear the table, though."

I open my mouth to argue, but then shut it again. I'm not sixteen anymore.

"Good boy," she says in that patronising manner grown-ups always have. "I've got to go. Edna's going to have my guts for garters.

Sylvia laughs. "Go. You don't want Edna sulking all afternoon."

Mary makes that snorting noise again and walks off, leaving me and Sylvia. I looked at her helplessly.

"First, we have to spring you out of here," she says immediately.

"You make it sound like a prison break. How do you know they'll let me go today?"

"Because you're being released into my care," she says smugly.

"I'm nineteen. I don't need to be released into anybody's care. They didn't try and help me when I was under eighteen. They can't make me accept help now."

Sylvia stops looking so smug. "Danny, the staff *knows* you. *I* know you. We've nursed you through three bouts of pneumonia, bronchitis, a stabbing, and this last time. You walked out every time social workers tried to get you into shelters and other schemes. For once in your life, accept that people want to help you."

"You think I trust anyone enough to help me? My parents threw me out when I was a kid." I hiss the angry words at her, stopping, embarrassed when my voice cracks.

I see the pity in her eyes and it makes me cringe, but she says, "Oh, baby, you aren't the only one. We've seen so many kids rejected by their mums and dads. Come home, Danny. Stay for dinner, stay for one night, if that's all you can manage. But let us help."

I stare at her for a long moment.

Chapter 9

The house is a surprise. Not that I'm sure what I was expecting. Maybe a large room in the back of an old lady's house. Instead, Sylvia shows me to a door down the side of the house.

"This was built as the granny annex for the people before us. We've been here for about thirty years. Mum and Dad never used it except to store junk, but when Allan died and Mum started taking on waifs and strays, she redecorated the place. It's not that big, but it's got a kitchen and a bathroom."

Sylvia's right. The place is tiny, but for someone like me, used to a hollow under a bush, it's a fucking mansion. The rooms are simply decorated, plain light walls and no pictures. Sylvia sees me looking around.

"You can put what you like on the walls. If you decide to stay, Mum asks that you help redecorate when you leave. Over the years, everybody has helped Mum prepare for the next person along."

There a small TV in one corner of the room, and.... I look closely... a PlayStation. Sylvia follows my wide-eyed gaze. "The games console was donated by kids in the local area. There are a few games in the cupboard."

"You trust me not to nick these and sell them?"

"You're not going to get a lot of money for them. It's not like they're new or anything. Why don't you leave your bag here and come and have dinner. Mum said it's ready." She holds up her phone.

"Your mum knows how to text?" I'm impressed. My gran could barely manage the house phone.

"She's learned over the years. Too many kids around for her not to have picked up a trick or two. If she offers to play *Crash Bandicoot* with you, on your head be it."

I look at her skeptically. "Your mum's a master at *Crash Bandicoot*?"

"Among other games. Don't you underestimate Mary Wilson. Too many people have done that, to their cost."

I mutter something that seems to satisfy Sylvia, and she leads me through the door to the rest of the house. I don't leave my bag, despite her suggestion I do so. The house smells just like mine used to before.... Angry at myself for being such a sap, I blink back tears. Mary's waiting in the kitchen for us, poking at something on the hob. She looks over her shoulder as we come in.

"Finally. I thought you'd got lost."

"I showed him around," Sylvia says easily enough. She doesn't sound bothered by her mum's snippiness.

"What do you think, young man?" Mary asks.

"It's very nice," I say politely.

She frowns. "Nice? Is that the best you can manage?"

I'm not sure what else I can say, but luckily

Sylvia comes to my rescue.

"Leave him alone, Mum. It's a lot to take in."

Mary harrumphs and points to the chair at the pine table. "Sit down, then, and I'll serve up. You must be starving."

Not really. I'm too nervous to be hungry, but I sit down anyway. Mary places a plate full of roast lamb, roast potatoes, Yorkshire pudding, and vegetables in front of me.

"Gravy?"

"Yeah."

"Yes, please," she says firmly.

"Huh? Oh, yes, please. Sorry." I'm going to have to remember my manners. Mum was never bothered by "yeah" and "nope," but Mary froths at the mouth every time I forget.

"Better. Eat up."

I eat—and eat—and eat, until I'm completely stuffed. I can barely manage half the plate because my stomach has shrunk during the illness, but something inside me rebels at leaving food like that, not knowing when I might see it again.

Sylvia lays a hand on my arm. "Don't make yourself sick, honey. If you want, we can cover it up and you can take it back to the flat."

"You don't mind?"

"Of course not," Mary says. "It's important you feel comfortable. Besides, you might get hungry in the night. Just make sure you return the plate washed, okay?"

The words are out of my mouth before I have time to think about them. "I thought you had a dishwasher."

"Call it a sign of goodwill," she says easily.

I nod slowly. The women have shown me more than enough goodwill. I can wash one plate. A yawn catches me by surprise. It's barely seven o'clock, yet I feel exhausted.

"Why don't you have an early night?" Sylvia starts wrapping my plate up in cling film.

"I...." I want to say no. I want to get up and run, run away from all these people pretending to be nice and ordering me around.

"Sleep, Danny. Tomorrow you'll feel better and more able to make a decision."

Mary sounds firm and I give in. I'm too fucking tired to care. I let Sylvia lead me back to the flat. The bed is already made up with some well-worn sheets. I wonder briefly how many people have slept in them and decide I don't care enough to ask.

Sylvia shows me the bathroom, complete with toothpaste and new toothbrush, and then leaves me to it with, "See you tomorrow evening. I'm working all day tomorrow."

I nod. Maybe I'll see her, maybe I won't. I'll think about it in the morning. "'Night, Sylvia. Thank you."

I take off my sweats and get under the duvet. The bed is firm and miles more comfortable than a hospital bed. I contemplate turning on the TV, and in mid-thought, I fall asleep.

A gentle knocking wakes me up. I sit up with a start, heart racing as I can't work out where I am.

"Danny, are you awake? I've brought you breakfast."

"Hold on." I skim into the joggers Sylvia brought me yesterday and then open the door from the house.

Mary's standing on the other side with a covered plate that smells suspiciously like bacon and eggs.

"Hi," I say breathlessly. "Um, good morning?" I add hastily as she starts to frown.

"Almost. It's two in the afternoon."

"It's 2:00 p.m.?" I stare at her. I've slept nearly seventeen hours.

"I was wondering if you'd left without saying good-bye, but the curtains were still closed from the outside, so I took the chance you were still asleep. Now, where would you like to eat breakfast? In the flat? Or in the kitchen with me? I'm just about to make a cup of tea."

"In the kitchen?" From the way she beams at me, that was the correct answer. "Can I just use the bathroom and I'll join you?"

Mary nods and turns away. In the daylight, I see scars on her wrists that I hadn't noticed before. I recognise those scars. She catches me looking and shrugs. "There were dark days," she says simply.

Suddenly overwhelmed again, I lean forwards and kiss her cheek. "I understand. I've had some of those myself." I have a matching set of scars—from the first bewildering months after Hopeless House—but I don't bother showing them. She probably already knows.

Her eyes gleam suspiciously before she heads for the kitchen.

I go for a piss and clean my teeth. I'd like a shower but there isn't time. I haven't got any clean clothes, so it doesn't take me long to finish up and join Mary in the kitchen.

Another full plate awaits me. Bacon, eggs, sausages, baked beans, and hash browns. There are tinned tomatoes, as well, but I wouldn't eat them in a million years. My granny ate those and they're all slimy and disgusting. I eat around them and try to ignore where the juice has soaked into the hash browns.

Mary drinks her tea and watches me, not bothering to start a conversation until I've finished. I do better this time, almost emptying the plate except for one sausage and the tomatoes.

"Do you want to take the plate back?" she asks.

I shake my head. "No, thank you. If you show me where the bin is, I'll clear the plate."

She points to a gray caddy on the windowsill. "Throw the food in that, rinse the plate, and put it in the dishwasher over there. There's the same arrangement in the flat."

"I have a dishwasher?" I hadn't noticed.

"If you stay you do," she says.

I sigh and look down at the table, noticing small holes in regular patterns. "I don't know what to do."

"No need to rush. Rest for a few days and then make a decision. Anyone can see you're still getting over the pneumonia."

"I'm fine," I say defensively.

"And I'm the Queen," Mary snaps back. "Look, we're not expecting you to make an immediate decision, but for heaven's sake, Danny, don't turn away help because of your pride. Have you looked outside today?"

I hadn't and only notice now it's tipping it down. Fuck, going back to the park would be a nightmare, not to mention I'd have to find some cardboard and get it back without it getting soggy.

"Curl up in bed for the afternoon and watch TV. You can play *Crash Bandicoot* with me later." Mary sees my face. "Sylvia's been telling tales, hasn't she?"

"She said you're a shark," I admit, getting up to clean my plate.

After that, I do as Mary suggests—curl up in bed and watch daytime TV. I can't believe they're still showing the same episodes of *Midsomer Murders.* I fall asleep just before the murderer is revealed, but it doesn't matter because I've seen it before.

Mary leaves me dinner again with a note that reads *Tomorrow you're making lasagne.*

That fills me with apprehension. The last time I cooked anything was in Food Tech six years ago, and it did not go well.

This time she's given me chicken and mashed potatoes. It's not my favourite, but I'm not arguing. I eat it all up and then wash the plate. There's no point running the dishwasher for one plate. As soon as I've done that I'm asleep again, and this time I don't wake up until morning.

For a few days, the pattern of my day revolves around mealtimes and my cooking lessons. Mary seems determined to teach me to cook. The results have been... interesting. I'm so tired cooking is all I can manage, and Mary and Sylvia don't seem to expect any more. Sylvia lets slip how pleased she is I am still here. I'm amazed myself, but fatigue has a lot to do with it.

Mary and Sylvia treat me well enough. I get told to eat, sleep, and shower. I point out to them I'm not three years old, but they just nod and wait until I've done whatever it is they want me to do. No amount of muttering or complaining changes their minds. I'm not strong enough to argue yet, but I will be. I'm frightened by how weak I've become. I'm nineteen years old and I have no strength at all. How close I've come to checking out is brought home when I catch another chest infection and have to see the doctor about more antibiotics. The doctor wants me to go back to hospital but Mary promises she will nurse me back to health. I sleep again, the cooking lessons suspended for now, and all thoughts of leaving are lost in feverish dreams. I'm not stupid enough to think I can survive this winter outside.

It's nearly Christmas before I'm back on my feet again. One afternoon Mary knocks at the flat door, as she always does. I asked her once why she doesn't just walk in. She gave me an odd look and said, "This is your home. You don't enter people's homes without knocking. It's not right." I don't really care, but maybe I will when I feel better.

"Hello, Danny. I'm going up to the top shop. Is there anything you want?"

The top shop is the local store. It's like the TARDIS from *Doctor Who*, apparently—small from the outside and a maze inside, full of everything you could ever need. I haven't actually got out of the flat to see it. I've been here a couple of months and spent most of it in bed.

"No, thanks." I am sacked out on the beanbag under a pink fleece blanket, watching *Dante's Peak*, and I have no intention of moving.

Mary looks disapproving for a minute; she's started to make noises about me helping her with the shopping and stuff. I play the tired card and sink further into the beanbag. Then she sighs and says, "Sylvia and I normally help at the local homeless shelter for Christmas Day. We don't bother with a Christmas dinner. Will you come with us?"

I'm irrationally disappointed. I've been looking forwards to a proper Christmas, my first in three years. I turn my attention back to the TV. "No, thanks. I've spent enough Christmases there."

"All the more reason you should come and help. Give back what you got from them," she says briskly.

I grit my teeth to keep the angry words from spilling out. "I don't feel well enough. Another time." I keep my attention focused on the TV rather than look at her.

"You need to get out, Danny. You're not sick

anymore, and being lazy won't help you get your strength back."

"I don't want to go back to the shelter."

Mary comes and sits on the sofa next to me. "Is that what's bothering you? Having to go back there?"

I nod but still won't look at her.

"Oh, Danny, you don't have to worry. They'll be thrilled to see you again. They know you're with me."

Startled, I look at her for the first time. In the background, the world is coming to an end, but I pay no attention. "You've talked about me?"

She nods. "Of course. I've worked with them for years. I probably met you before, although I don't remember." She looks vaguely embarrassed.

"I don't remember you either," I admit. "Maybe we missed each other. I wasn't there all the time."

"Well, they're pleased you're all right. They were worried when you stopped coming in for meals. I told them you were in hospital and now with me. Greg wants to know when you'll be coming in to see him."

"You think they would mind if I went back?"

She smiles at me. "I think they'd be delighted. Now, I'm going up to the shop. When I get back you can help me cook dinner."

I groan loudly. "Do I have to?"

"Yes, you do. Time you were back on your feet again instead of watching this trash."

"It's not trash."

"I don't care. I've let you get away with being lazy for far too long. Rules, remember?"

I'd hoped she'd forgotten the damn rules. Saying as much earns me a whup around the head.

"Hey!" I clutch at my head and stare indignantly at her. To my surprise, Mary isn't smiling at me.

"Danny, you've been sick. Sicker than most of the kids we've had here, and I've let things slide. But this isn't a holiday or a hotel. I told you that in the beginning. If you stay here, you have to help me and find work. You've been here for weeks, and it's time you pulled your weight."

Her face is so serious it makes me sit up. "Are you going to throw me out?"

"Not yet. As I said, you've been sick. But staying in here will just make you depressed, and that's no good for you. Now get your shoes on and take a walk up to the top shop with me."

"I don't have a coat." It's fucking freezing out there. I know, because I saw the frost on the fence outside the window.

"Yes, you do." Mary gets up and goes to the small cupboard by the front door. She produces a black coat and the trainers. The coat is puffy, the sort of thing I'd have worn to school, protesting all the time.

I'm not going to get away with that today, so I sigh pitifully and take the trainers. I've lost a lot of weight, and my feet slip and slide in the shoes. Mary notices. "We'll get you another pair tomorrow."

"You don't have to do that," I say, embarrassed she saw, but she shakes her head.

"You can't wear badly fitting shoes all the time. You'll get blisters."

The cold air is a shock after the heat of the flat. Mary and Sylvia keep the place almost too warm, and I guess I've got spoilt in the short time I've been there. I shuffle beside her up the road. I'm shocked to find the short walk up the hill is almost more than I can manage.

In the shop, which is dark and crowded, I lean against a wall to recover. Mary is chatting away to a middle-aged guy, Barry, who turns out to be the owner. He eyes me appraisingly.

"You're the latest, are you?"

I nod. The latest in a long line of lame ducks.

"What's your name?"

"Danny." It sounds more defensive than I mean it to.

"Good to meet you, Danny. Glad to see you on your feet."

I look over to Mary, who shrugs. "Barry's met most of my guests. He was wondering why he hadn't seen you."

He gives me that long appraising look, and I have a fair idea what's coming next.

"You look after Mary and Sylvia, and don't give them any hassle, you hear me?"

And there it is... the "hurt my friend and I'll hurt you" speech.

"I won't. I promise." I don't want to hurt the only two people who've looked after me in a long time. I don't think of Harry. I *never* think of Harry if I can help it.

Mary ignores Barry and points at the sweet

counter. "Let's treat ourselves. What do you want, Danny?"

I walk over to look. "Mars bar, please."

She sees my glance at the fridge and rolls her eyes. "Go on, then. Just this once. You can pick whilst I get the beans."

I add a can of Coke to the sweets and then wait for her to complete the rest of her shopping. As Barry doesn't seem inclined to talk, I wander over to the magazine rack. I don't recognise any of the faces on the covers, and I realise how out of touch I am for my age.

"Do you want one?" Mary calls, pointing at the magazines.

I shake my head. "No, thanks." I see the look of approval on Barry's face and I'm tempted to change my mind. Fuck him. I don't need his approval.

But Mary's already paying and I know it would look petty.

The walk back is easier, but by the time we get there I'm ready to sit down again. Mary has other ideas, though.

As we go in through her front door, she says, "Put your coat and shoes away, and then come in the kitchen. You can have a cuppa while you peel the spuds." I huff, but she wags her finger. "You heard what I said earlier, young man. No lazing around now. You aren't sick any longer."

"I'm tired," I protest.

"Tough." She turns her back on me and heads for the kitchen.

I grumble under my breath.

"I heard that," she yells.

Inside the flat, I slam the connecting door to make me feel better. I'm shattered. All I want to do is climb into bed and fall asleep, but I've got a feeling she'll drag me out of bed if I do. Like an obedient little school boy, I put away my coat and trainers, and then go back to Mary before she comes looking for me..

Chapter 10

A few days before Christmas, Sylvia and Mary discover it's my birthday. December 21. Stupid time to have a birthday. Everyone is running around trying to get Christmas ready and no one wants to be bothered with holding a party or getting birthday presents. Mum used to try and make up for it by holding my parties at different times of the year. I used to come home from school and discover it was designated party day. It was a strange thing to do, but that was my mum.

I can see by the looks on their faces that Sylvia and Mary take birthdays seriously, and sure enough, I'm called into the kitchen to find a chocolate birthday cake and a wrapped present.

Sylvia hands over the present with an embarrassed look on her face. "Here. We didn't know what to get you."

I mumble a thank-you and stare at it for a moment.

"You can open it. It won't bite," she teases.

It's a couple of DVDs. The shape had already given it away. It's two films I haven't seen. They'd come out after Dad kicked me out.

"Thank you." I'm really touched they took the time to buy me something.

"We got you socks and pants, as well, but we didn't wrap those up," Mary says. She hands over a bag from Marks & Spencer.

I'm just as grateful for those, even if the thought of her buying me underwear is icky. I give them both a hug and then sit down to eat the cake. It is as rich and gooey as it looks, and I eat half of it without even thinking. I'm always hungry at the moment.

"Greg wishes you a happy birthday as well." Sylvia hands over another small package.

I blink at her. "He knew it was my birthday?"

"He did once I told him."

Unwrapping the package reveals a pack of razors, shaving cream, and a small bottle. I squint at it.

"It's supposed to soothe your skin after shaving," Sylvia supplies helpfully.

I run my hand over the scruff on my face. I've never grown a proper beard, but I haven't even bothered to tidy it up in months. Once it got past the itching stage, I stopped caring.

"I suppose this is a hint," I say drily.

Sylvia shakes her head. "Take it as an order."

"This concept of being allowed to get on with my life... it's not quite true, is it?"

"With help. You can get along with help." Mary hands me another can of pop.

"I'm twenty years old today." I point out. "Most kids are managing fine by themselves at this age."

"Most kids are still slumming it off Mum and Dad at twenty," Sylvia says. "Now stop whinging and go shave."

"Yes, Mum," I say sarcastically. "Can I have some more cake?"

"When you've shaved," they say in chorus.

I scowl at them. "This is a setup, isn't it?"

"Don't know what you mean." Mary makes a shooing motion.

I give up and head for my bathroom. Of all the amazing things about having my own place, number one is the bed and number two is the bathroom. I have a bathroom with hot running water and no one wanting to share it or me. Sometimes I stand under the shower for fifteen minutes, just because I can.

The mirror reflects a harsh truth. I look ten years older than my two decades. Being ill for more than two months, I've lost so much weight my face is almost skeletal, and the gingerish facial hair is now more than scruff. My beard is still several shades darker than my blond hair. My eyes are sunk deep, the black smudges underneath doing them no favours.

"Jesus, you look like death warmed up," I mutter.

It takes me some time to shave. There are two reasons for this: one, I'm tired, and my hand is shaking; and two, I'm absolutely crap at shaving. Prior to leaving home, Dad had thrown an electric shaver at me and left me to get on with it. I'd used it about once every three months. After that, shaves were few and far between and normally done by the barber who came to the drop-in centre.

Eventually it is done, and with minimal blood

loss on my part. I grin at my reflection in relief. I leave the mess in the sink and lie down on my bed, and within seconds, I'm asleep.

The next day I'm praised for my efforts with the razor and then given a telling off for the state of the bathroom, but they don't make any mention of the fact I'd gone back to bed. Sylvia is working up to Christmas Eve so she can spend Christmas Day at the shelter. It doesn't sound like much of a holiday to me, but when I say so, she laughs.

"You're right, but I like being at the shelter. I feel useful. Otherwise Mum and I just sit around staring at each other."

"When was your brother killed?" I ask, a horrible suspicion dawning.

"Just before Christmas," she says, her face pinched.

"I'm so sorry, Sylvia." I feel uncomfortable and sad for her loss, but also angry. I'm not a plaything for her to use as a substitute for her brother.

She smiles sadly at me. "It was a long time ago, duck. We deal. I know this must be difficult for you, but it keeps Mum happy, and she feels Allan's life wasn't wasted."

"I'm not him," I blurt out.

"No, you're not." She looks at me seriously. "I will keep telling you that over and over again. You aren't Allan, and none of the kids who have passed through our doors are him. We aren't looking for another son and brother."

"What happened after he died? Where is your dad?" I hope she doesn't mind me asking questions.

"Dad died of a heart attack a year after Allan passed. He never really recovered from Allan's death."

"I saw the scars on your mum's wrists."

Sylvia nods. "It was about a week after Dad died. I was at work. I got a call that Mum was downstairs in A&E. She'd waited until I went out and then tried to slit her wrists. Fortunately, she fainted before she did any real damage, and a neighbour found her.

"After that, she was in a psychiatric ward for months. She just shut down."

I stare at her. I thought my story was bad enough, but this is tragic. I have no idea what to say to her.

Sylvia catches my expression. "As I said, a long time ago. We have helped so many kids since then, and we're still in contact with most of them."

"You never got married?"

She shook her head. "Never found the right man."

"That's...."

"Pathetic, I know. But honestly, I don't really mind. If I was going to do the family thing, it would have happened. I have a good career, and I love Mum and you lot. I never really wanted kids of my own."

"Nor me." I shudder at the thought of babies and then blush. What would I have to offer kids anyway?

Sylvia laughs but she doesn't give me the usual, "You're young, you'll change your mind," which I used to get from my mum. "We're going to the shelter early so we can set up for the lunch."

I bite the inside of my lip. I really don't want to go back to the shelter.

"You don't have to go, but I think you'd find it helpful," she says.

"Helpful?"

She takes my hand and leads me to the sofa. As we sit, she says, "You still haven't made up your mind about staying, have you?"

"I'm still here," I mutter.

"In body, not in spirit. Once you relax and stop thinking it's a dream, or we're about to throw you out, then you'll feel better."

I sigh, because she's right. It's not that I'm not happy—kind of—here, and I feel better than I have in years with the good food and a proper bed, but I keep waiting for the other shoe to drop. "I don't mean to be ungrateful."

"You're not ungrateful. You're suspicious, and rightly so. Even we see how odd it looks. Two old biddies taking young people into their home."

"You're not old," I say automatically and see I've said the right thing.

"You're a good boy, Danny. We were lucky to find you."

To her surprise—and mine—I lean forwards and kiss her cheek. "I think it's the other way around."

"Get on with you. Now Mum isn't going to hassle you for at least an hour."

Great. I can play on the PlayStation for a while. That woman makes my score look embarrassing. I haven't spent as much time as I expected on the PlayStation. Partly because I've been ill, but mainly because I don't have the concentration. I fall asleep watching TV. The doctor says my body's recovering, that I'll feel better soon. I hope so, because I feel like shite.

I spend an hour playing *Crash Bandicoot* and then I go in search of Mary to see what she wants me to cook. Oh yes, the cooking lessons don't stop because it's Christmas. Yesterday she gave me a break because it was my birthday, but the day before, I cooked mince pies. I hate mince pies, and I hate them even more now I've spent hours filling that slimy, yucky stuff into the pastry cases.

I knock on the kitchen door. Mary looks up from the table, where she's poring over a recipe book.

"Afternoon, Danny. Don't you look handsome?"

I resist the urge to hide my chin. "It feels better."

"Clean-shaven suits you much better," she says.

"I like my men with a beard," I shoot back and then hold my breath, wondering if I've gone too far.

Mary laughs and I relax. "Ooh no, all that beard rash."

"Mary!" I exclaim, because no... just no.

She chuckles again and points at the book. "I'll stop embarrassing you now. What shall we cook today? I'm all out of ideas."

Relieved to change the subject, I point at the wok hanging up with the other saucepans. "I'd like to make a stir-fry. I haven't eaten Chinese since I left home."

She tilts her head. "I'd need to get the ingredients. Tell you what. Sylvia is finishing early today. How about I see if she would like to go out for a meal?"

"You want to take me to a restaurant?" I ask dubiously.

"Yes. Why? Do you have a problem with that?"

"No," I say hastily, "I just didn't know if you'd want to be seen with me." My voice trails off and I look away. I don't see Mary get up and come over to me.

"Are you worried about what you look like?" she asks kindly.

I nod, because if I was in her shoes, I wouldn't want to be seen with me.

"You look fine to me," she says briskly, "but if you want, we can go out and get your hair cut. You'll need to anyway, for the job interviews."

"Job interviews? What job interviews?"

"The ones you're going to after the New Year. Come on, now."

Before I even have time to think, Mary is getting her coat and bag. I get my coat and trainers and follow her out the door. The woman is like a tsunami. She never gives me time to think about anything. Perhaps that's the best way to deal with losers like me.

My hair, dark blond when it isn't filthy dirty, lies in a circle around my feet. The barber, "Mick, don't take it," took one look at my hairstyle and reached for the scissors. I was thinking a trim; he was thinking a massacre.

"Now, that's better, young man," he booms.

I look at myself in the mirror. "Fuck," I mouth. I don't recognise the boy in the mirror. I haven't seen him for years.

He frowns at me. "No need for that language."

"Sorry, no, I meant... I can't believe it's me."

Mick's face softens and he nods. "You look your age now. You're quite the looker under all that hair. Too thin, but not bad-looking."

I know from Mary's introduction that he knows I'm homeless and she's paying for the haircut, but he doesn't treat me any the worse for it.

"The last time my hair was this short was 1999," I say.

"You didn't get it cut at all?"

"Sometimes, but not much. It kept my head warm. Some men preferred to be bald, but I kept mine." I don't apologise for the way I looked, and from his expression he doesn't expect me to.

"You'll find it easier to look after now," is all he says.

I run my fingers through the strands, earning myself a smack on the hand.

"Leave it alone." He fusses again until my hair is neat and tidy once more. "I can't have you leaving my shop looking like a bum. I've got a reputation to maintain."

"I am a bum," I point out.

"You're one of Mary's kids. You're not a bum anymore."

Mary comes into the shop at that point. She left me at Mick's mercy whilst she went shopping. She does a double take when she sees me.

"My goodness, who is this handsome young man?"

I feel my cheeks heat up. "Mary!"

"You look amazing. You're going to have all the young men after you."

"*Mary!*" I squirm on the seat and daren't look at Mick.

He laughs at my discomfiture. "And some of the old men."

I snap my head up. He catches my eye in the mirror. "You need to be more observant, son."

He turns, and I see a rainbow flag on his bicep. I hadn't noticed it amongst all the other tattoos making up one large sleeve.

Mary joins in his laughter, and I want the world to swallow me whole.

"Come on, Danny, let's go buy some clothes."

I frown. I'm wearing the joggers Sylvia gave me the day I came out of hospital. I alternate between these and a couple of other pairs. "I don't need more clothes."

"You at least need a pair of jeans, and I can't buy those for you," she says.

Mick pats my arm. "You seem like a decent young man. Mary knows you'll pay her back when you can. Let her do this for you now."

I turn in my seat and look at them both. He towers over her—he's at least six foot—with huge muscled arms. They stare back at me, kind expressions on their faces. They don't show any sign of pitying me. That's what I hate. I nod slowly. "One pair, and you keep a note of what you're spending. I'll find some way of paying you back."

"Are you any good with a drill?" she asks hopefully.

"I did some work at the shelter," I say. "It depends what you need doing."

Mary shakes her head. "We'll see. I've got a few jobs around the house, but I'm not letting you use power tools without supervision."

I feel useless and inadequate again, but I don't think she notices. We say good-bye to Mick and head towards the shopping centre. The choice is limited for men in my town, and I'm not hopeful of finding anything I like. I used to loiter in the centre when I needed somewhere warm to go, so I know what's around. Most days the security guard threw me out, but sometimes one of them would buy me a hot chocolate and let me stay.

We head towards the only real shop that sells clothes for men under fifty. I hesitate at the door. I've been thrown out of here more than once.

Mary notices my hesitation. "Danny, what's wrong?"

"I'm not welcome in here," I whisper.

"Ah." She nods and says, "That was before. Come on."

I follow her because what else can I do? I look around, but no one pays me any attention. I see the snooty bitch with the long, dyed-blonde hair and too-small clothes. She's called security more than once, but she doesn't even raise her head.

"See?" Mary says, staying close to my side. "No one cares now."

They don't, but I still feel out of place.

"Think of it like this," Mary says. "You're Julia Roberts, she's the saleswoman on Rodeo Drive."

"Huh?"

"*Pretty Woman*?"

Mary sees my blank look and sighs. "Julia Roberts is a hooker and gets picked up by Richard Gere, who showers her with clothes and expensive jewelry. She gets told to leave one store and then the hotel manager helps her. She goes back to the shop and gloats over the shop assistant for the sales commission she's lost."

I give her a look. "So let me see. I'm a hooker and you're a... what? A kerb crawler?"

"Yes. No. Shut up!"

I don't get my Julia Roberts moment, but I do get the chance to make Mary blush. That works for me.

I find some black jeans that fit. Mary refused to buy the ones that were below my hips. I thought they looked great. She thought they looked obscene. As she was paying, I didn't get a chance to argue.

As we leave the shop, the snooty bitch looks up and catches my eye. I see her frown as if she recognises me but doesn't know from where. I look away—there's no point causing a scene.

The shopping centre is heaving with people as it's three days before Christmas, and it reminds me of something that's been preying on my mind.

"Mary?"

She looks up from where she's been eyeing a purple scarf in one of the stalls. "Yes?"

"I can't buy you and Sylvia a present."

She frowns at me. "I don't expect one. Neither does Sylvia."

"But Christmas is a time for presents."

"Christmas is a time for loving each other. Presents are secondary."

I shuffle from foot to foot. "But...."

Mary squeezes my shoulder. "You have no reason to feel bad. We have bought you small gifts. Things you need, that's all." She looks at me closely. "Do you want to go home?"

I nod. Suddenly the crowd and the decorations, the music and the fake Christmas spirit—everything's getting just a bit much. I need to go home and hide, like I used to under the bush in the park. The temptation to run back to the park is overwhelming.

Mary takes my arm as if she knows what's running through my head. "Come on, sweetheart, I think we could do with a cuppa at home."

I swallow hard and let her take me home, because I know if I think too much, I'll be gone.

Chapter 11

At home I wrap my hands around a mug as Mary bustles around. She's very quiet and leaves me to my thoughts, which I appreciate.

"I want to change my name," I say suddenly.

"What?"

"I want to change my name. I don't want to be Danny anymore."

"All right." She sits down at the table and looks at me expectantly. "What do you want to be called instead?"

"David Miles." I've been thinking about it since my birthday.

"That's a nice name. Any middle name?"

I shake my head. "Just that." It's close enough to my name that people might remember it.

"We can do this legally if you want, but we can start calling you David now."

"Please." I love Mary for not questioning it. My dad would have gone ballistic at any thought of changing my name. Mind you, if he hadn't thrown me out, I would never have had to change my name.

"Well, David, once we've had the tea, you can watch TV, then we'll go out for a meal."

I nod. I need a break before I face the world

again.

Christmas Day

My heart is pounding in my chest and sweat is prickling my palms as I approach the shelter on Christmas Day. It's been several months since I've been there. Being in hospital and then at Mary's, I've had no reason to go for my regular meals. Mary and Sylvia flank me as we walk in the door. I wonder if it's to give me support or to keep me from running away. Maybe a bit of both.

"Dan-David. It's really good to see you again." Ben comes towards me with a look of pleasure on his face.

"Ben. It's good to see you too." He doesn't hug me or touch me. It occurs to me the only time he's touched me was when I got stabbed. He held my hand and didn't let go until the ambulance arrived. I still feel uncomfortable with much physical contact. Mary and Sylvia are wonderful and tactile, but sometimes even their touches are too much.

"Do you want to help with the spuds, David?" Ben asked.

I'm daunted by the amount of potatoes that need peeling, but Sylvia soon comes in to help me. Five minutes later, a man I don't recognise comes and sits down next to me.

"Hi, my name's Jack. Ben suggested you might need help." He has a soft American accent.

I look at him carefully. He doesn't look like a

user, so I assume he's a volunteer, and he confirms that when he says his stepsister and stepmother are on their way in to help.

"My name's... David." I don't stumble exactly but I have to think about it.

"Jack Cooper."

I nod as I reach for another potato. "You said that already."

He flushes, and I feel oddly guilty for embarrassing him. "I forgot. I've got the attention span of a gnat."

"You work here?" I ask.

"No, it's my first time."

I have a decision to make. I can either tell him who I am or make a fresh start. Jack doesn't know me from Adam. Danny is a homeless bum; David is a young man with potential. "This is my first time as well." I can feel Sylvia's gaze on me, but she doesn't contradict my lie.

"You'll enjoy today, Jack," she says easily.

He beams at her. He's got a huge smile, and I feel the world slide out from underneath me. I recognise that smile. I used to see it every day as he came towards me. Jack might have an American accent, but his name is Harry. He doesn't look anything like my Harry, but I'm sure I'm right. His brown hair is cropped short with a spiky top, and his green eyes.... I can't look too closely, but he seems to be wearing blue contact lenses. It's him, though, I know it.

"I'm sure I will. We're just over here for a couple of weeks and thought we'd do something useful."

I frown. "You're from America?" I mean, I knew he wasn't from America.

Jack shakes his head. "Yes and no. I lived here until just over a year ago. I moved to America when my mum died. I had to go and live with my dad."

"Your mum died?" Well, that explains why he disappeared from my life, although not the suddenness.

"Yeah." Jack looks away from me and I wonder if he's trying not to cry. "Car accident on the way home from work."

"I'm sorry." I mean it. I feel sad at the thought of that lovely lady dying. She'd been so kind to me.

He looks miserable for a moment, and I want to give him a hug. "Me too. One minute I had a home and a boyfriend, and the next I was living in North Carolina and listening to Pastor Charlie thundering about faggots for an hour and a half every Sunday."

I winced. "That must have been hard."

"Yeah," he says shortly. He carries on with peeling the potatoes, and for a moment there is silence.

"Why does your dad live in America?"

"He's American. He met my mum when she worked in America. After they divorced, she brought me to England and he stayed in America and got remarried."

I had forgotten that detail about him. I remembered he spent his holidays in America, but not why.

"So what happened to your boyfriend?" I ask, making my voice casual. Too casual, perhaps, because Sylvia is looking at me out of the corner of her eye.

"I didn't see him again, and I couldn't contact him to tell him what happened."

"Couldn't you ring him?"

"He didn't have a phone."

Jack looks up at the derisive noise I make.

"Not everyone is lucky enough to have a good home," he says defensively, "And my dad took me to my gran's."

I want to say he could have left a fucking *note*, but he'd lost his mum, and probably hadn't even thought about it.

"You have a strong accent for someone who's only been there a year," Sylvia says.

"I lived there for ten years before we moved to England," Jack says as he chops a potato. "I can switch between the accents depending on where I am. It saved me getting teased at school. I guess I didn't think about it this visit. No arsehole... revolting kids calling me names."

And suddenly I'm listening to my Harry. I drop the potato in shock at the sweet tones of my boy.

"That's quite a change," Sylvia says.

"I change my name and my accent. I'm Harry over here and Jack in America. Jonathan Henry, really."

Sylvia frowns. "Isn't that confusing?"

"Yeah, but I can't be Harry in America. God, all the Prince Harry jokes. And I was Jack before, but when I went to school here, there were four Jacks in the class already, so I became Harry."

"How are we doing?" Ben interrupts the explanation.

"Nearly done," Sylvia says cheerfully.

Ben nudges her shoulder. "I can't believe you're doing the potatoes."

"And why's that?" she asks indignantly.

"You? In the kitchen? I thought hell would have to freeze over first."

I look at Sylvia curiously. "You don't cook?" It suddenly occurs to me I've never actually seen her cook. Mary cooks. I cook with Mary's supervision. But Sylvia has never cooked. I thought it was because Sylvia worked long enough hours. It didn't occur to me she couldn't cook. "Is that why Mary is teaching me to cook?"

Sylvia chuckles and Ben rolls his eyes.

"Mary teaches everyone to cook. She failed with Sylvia so she's determined that everyone else who comes through her doors will learn to cook."

"I burn everything," Sylvia confides.

"Or gives us food poisoning. Do you remember the chicken?" Ben says.

Sylvia bursts out laughing, and for a moment I am envious of their shared history.

Jack looks at me curiously. "So you live with Mary and Sylvia? And Ben lived there too?"

"Mary has a flat she rents out," Ben says easily, and I nod in agreement.

"Oh. Cool. I'm going to be renting at college."

"You're going to college?" I ask.

"In the fall. Stanford. I want to be a lawyer."

"Wow." I'm impressed. Then it hits me. He's

going back to America. "You're not coming back?"

Jack shakes his head. "There's nothing for me here. Most of my relatives live in America, and I didn't really have any friends here."

"What about your old boyfriend?" I ask, trying not to sound aggressive.

Jack takes the last potato and stares at it. "I hope I see him before I go. I might... I hope I see him today. He might not want to see me again."

"Was he homeless?" Sylvia asks gently.

At Jack's nod, Ben squeezes his shoulder. "We get all sorts in here on Christmas Day. What's his name?"

"Danny. His name was Danny. He used to live in the Rec."

I feel Sylvia's and Ben's eyes pinning me where I sit, but I keep my eyes on the potato I'm peeling.

"Do you know him?" Jack asks, and I can hear the hope in his voice.

"I know him," Ben admits, "but we haven't seen him for a while. Last I heard he was in hospital."

Jack drops the potato he was peeling. "In hospital. What for?"

"I don't know." Of course Ben knew, but he wasn't going to tell Jack. This way, he had let the boy down gently and not given away too many secrets.

"Probably pneumonia. Danny was prone to that." Jack drops the last potato in the saucepan of water.

I swallow hard at the realization he remembers something like that.

"All done. Excellent. Sylvia, that's your kitchen

duties done. You boys can help me cook."

I groan loudly. Jack laughs and the subject is changed.

For the next couple of hours, Ben works us too hard to talk much. As the users stream in, men and women and a few children, we're kept busy dealing with their needs. I was on tenterhooks that someone would recognise me and give me away with a simple *Danny*, but for some reason, introducing myself as David is enough. The new clothes, short hair, and no scraggly beard is enough for people to see David, not Danny.

Ben and I cook dinner, with Jack as our slave. At least that's what Ben says. In reality, Ben does the cooking, I do what he tells me, and Jack, well, Jack spends a lot of time staring at me.

"He likes you," Ben says quietly as Jack takes in a tray of roast potatoes.

"Huh?"

"Don't give me that. He likes you. Are you going to tell him you're Danny?"

I shake my head. "Danny is dead."

"You think he won't find out one day?" Ben looks disapproving. He scowls at me as he dishes up the rest of the potatoes.

"Jack's going back to America after Christmas. I'm never going to see him again."

"Then don't you owe it to him to be honest? Give him some closure on his first love?"

Something digs into the palm of my hand. I look down to discover I'm holding on to a fork the wrong way and the tines are digging in. I discovered the spokes were called tines when I got a lecture from Mary on the correct cutlery to use. Seriously? I'm twenty years old and need a lecture on knives and forks?

Back to the problem at hand.

"If I tell him, then Danny never dies. He'll always view me with pity, just like the rest of you do."

"I don't pity you."

"Yes, you do."

"*I* don't pity you. I'm one of Mary's kids, remember?"

I look at Ben, startled, the echo of a conversation coming back to me. "You tried to tell me about Mary before, didn't you?"

He nods, but there's no chance to talk anymore because Jack comes back in for more potatoes. He obviously picks up on the tension, because he hangs about by the door.

"Is everything all right?" he asks.

Ben huffs out a breath and hands him another large covered serving dish of roasties. "It's fine. Da...." I wait for him to blow my cover. I can see him thinking about it. "David and I will bring in the rest."

Jack leaves after casting one last look at me.

"You need to tell him," Ben says insistently.

"There's no need. I won't see him again."

"Then there's no reason not to tell him."

I shake my head. "Leave it. He's just met David. He doesn't need to meet that loser, Danny."

"You were never a loser," Ben says quietly.

"Yes, I was... I am."

"One day this will come back to bite you on the

arse," Ben warns.

I shrug it off. He's worrying for nothing.

There's about a hundred people at the first sitting. I know Ben expects more later, and he's kept back food for them. We make sure all the users—Ben calls them clients and scolds me when I call them anything different—are fed, then we sit down. Jack sits next to me, pressed up tight. Occasionally he brushes his hand over my thigh. It's something I'm going to have to deal with soon, but not with his family sitting there.

Partway through, Santa Claus comes in with gifts for everyone. Sylvia told me last night that a local company had coughed up enough to provide a simple present for everyone and a little more for the kids. The looks on some of their faces, adult and child, is enough.

Many leave after the meal, the volume of people and noise too much for them. I watch Ben as he speaks to each and every one of them. Ben had always been there for me, even when I hadn't wanted his help. I'd seen it as interference then. God, I'd been a stupid moron.

I retreat to the kitchen to clear up. Even with the dishwashers there's a lot to do. I can't pinpoint the moment when I know Jack's watching me. It's like a gradual feeling.

"Going to help me or just laze around?" I ask as I stack the plates by the sink.

"I'll help."

"You wash, I'll dry. I know where they go."

"You've been here before?"

"A couple of times." I speak without thinking

and I can't remember if I'd said this was my first time or not.

"It's been better than last Christmas."

I am about to make a snide remark about mine being worse, and then I remember. I'm David now, and twelve months ago he'd just lost his mum.

"It was good of you all to give up your Christmas to help." Isn't that what they always say?

He nods. "I think I'll do it again. I liked helping, and the clients were great, except that random dude with the umbrella." Jack frowns. "I've got bruises where he poked me."

I laugh out loud. "You should have been quicker with his cup of tea, then."

Jack scowls at me. "For that, you can wash." He throws the soapy dishcloth at me.

I throw it back, soaking his T-shirt.

His eyes widen. "Oh, it's like that, is it?"

The next thing I know, I'm covered in soap bubbles he's scooped from the sink. The only thing I can do is behave like the mature man. I scoop my hand through the water and splash him. It disintegrates from there, and before long the kitchen is covered in soap bubbles and water.

"What the hell is going on?" Sylvia shrieks.

We stop and turn to her, Jack with his hand in the water, ready for the next throw.

She looks at us both, and then slowly around the kitchen. "Is there any reason the kitchen now looks like a swimming pool?"

"Er...." Jack looks at me. "Got a reason?"

I shook my head. "Not a good one."

"I suggest you mop up the mess and do the washing up before Ben gets back in here, otherwise he will hang, draw, and quarter you both."

"Yes, Sylvia. Sorry."

"Yes, ma'am." Jack seems a lot less worried about the threat of Ben's wrath than I am. He looks at me and grins when she walks out of the room. "Do you know where the mop is?"

I don't, but with a minor bit of exploration, we find two mops and start clearing the large expanse of soaking-wet floor. It takes us nearly an hour to finish the washing up. I get the feeling we're being left on our own as punishment for the water fight. Jack is cheerful, keeping up a steady chatter, mainly about his life back in America. It's mindless and I listen with half an ear as I wash the dishes. He's living the kind of life I would have had if it hadn't all gone shit-shaped. Despite the Bible-thumpers, he seems a lot happier in America than he was in England. I'm glad at least one of us is happy.

"Have you finished?" Ben asks, poking his head around the door.

"Nearly," Jack says with a sigh of relief.

"Great, because the next sitting will be in soon."

Jack's face falls. "You're joking."

I shake my head. "Nope. We have to do dinner in two sittings because of space."

Jack looks at the pile of plates he's just dried. "We have to do this all again."

"Yep." Ben sounds positively gleeful.

"Fuck!"

"Language!" Mary chides as she comes into the kitchen. "My turn to get the dinner ready. You boys can have a break. I have new helpers."

Hard on her heels are Jack's stepmother and stepsister. I can't remember their names, but I don't care. I'm out of that kitchen for a while. I look over to Jack. "Coming?"

"Hell, yes." Jack virtually pushes me out of the door in his haste.

"Be back in half an hour," Ben says. "We'll need help serving and clearing up."

I nod, more fatigued than I'm letting on, although I get the feeling I've not hidden it that well when Sylvia comes up to me.

"Do you need to go home?" she asks.

"No. I can stay."

"Go and get some fresh air. Jack, David's been ill, so if he tells you he's all right, he's lying."

"Sylvia!" I yelp, embarrassed at her blatant betrayal and worried Jack might connect the dots.

Jack casts a worried look at me. "Are you okay, man?"

I sigh. "Yeah, I'm fine. I'm just tired."

"It's not raining, so let's go out. We could sit in the park for a bit."

It's not hard to guess his intent. He's still looking for Danny.

"If you want." I haven't been in the park for months, but I know I have to make my peace with it.

The weather has other ideas. As we reach the door, I see it's chucking down rain.

"What do we do now?" Jack asks as he stares at

the rain.

The park is out. I'm relieved. I don't think I could have hidden my reaction to being in the place where we had loved. "We can hide in the office for a while."

"You grab some Cokes and I'll get those biscuits." Jack heads for the tins of biscuits stacked in the corner.

The office is crowded and the chairs are as comfortable as sitting on spikes, but there's Internet on the computer and Jack wants to show me some game or other. I spend half an hour watching him play. He's excited and happy, and I'm just pleased to be in his company again. I almost kiss him but hold back. He doesn't know David, and he's still looking for Danny. I look up from the screen at one point to see him staring at me with obvious interest, and the urge to tell him the truth is hot on my tongue.

But still I hold back.

Chapter 12

The long day takes a lot out of me, and I'm in bed before nine. I sleep almost fifteen hours, waking up just before midday. I'm grateful Mary and Sylvia let me sleep, and even more grateful when I realise they aren't going to force me to do anything else. After wearily managing a shower, I head for the sofa and watch TV. I swear they're the same programmes I watched four years ago.

I fall asleep watching *Stuart Little*, and wake up to the sound of a gentle knock at the front door. I frown. Nobody ever knocks at the front door. Nobody ever visits me. The only people who visit me are Mary and Sylvia, and they come in via the house door.

My visitor is Jack, smiling hesitantly on the doorstep.

"Hey," he says.

"Hi." I smile back, the effect ruined by the loudest yawn ever. My jaw cracks as I try to hold back the yawn.

"You look like shite," he says.

"Thanks." I don't need to be told that by the hot guy.

Jack flushes. "I didn't mean it like that."

"How did you mean it, then? Do you want to

come in?" I stand back and wave vaguely at the sofa.

"Yeah. Nice place," he says as he looks around.

"It is." It's a fucking palace as far as I'm concerned, but it's not the place that's so important. It's the love and care from two complete strangers—angels—that I have missed for so long.

"So Mary's what... your foster mum?"

"Kind of." I don't want to go into details.

Fortunately Jack seems to pick up on my mood and drops the subject. "I wondered if you want to go down to the pub."

I blink. At twenty years old I have never been to the pub—ever. I wasn't able to get away with it when I was still at home, and since I turned eighteen, I've not been in a position to go drinking. I saw the effect of alcohol on some of the other men in the shelter and avoided it. I'm about to say yes when I think of another problem.

"I can't." I frantically try to think of a reasonable excuse other than I'm skint, but I can't.

"No money?"

I nod.

"No worries. My treat. You can pay next time."

"I thought you were going home."

"I am. When I come over, I'll hunt you up for a return drink."

I can't think of another excuse, so I nod. "I ought to tell Mary."

Jack smiles at me, and my stomach flips a little more. "Cool."

When I knock on the door of Mary's lounge

and explain Jack's plan, she beams at me.

"That's sounds wonderful, dear. Just what you need after a day of lazing around."

"Would you like to come with us?" I ask, feeling I ought to ask.

To my relief she shakes her head. "After yesterday, I need a rest with my feet up. You go and have fun."

"Bye." As I close the door, I hear her call my name. I open the door again. "Yes?"

She's fumbling with her handbag. "Here, take some money."

I shake my head. "I don't want to take that. Jack says he'll pay."

"Nonsense. You have to pay your own way."

Reluctantly I take the twenty-pound note from her. "We've got to get my benefits sorted out."

"After the New Year. Now go on, have some fun."

"Thanks, Mary." I'm all choked up again.

She waves a hand at me. "Go on, before your date gets bored and runs away."

"It's not a date."

Mary purses her lips. "Oh really? So the boy you meet yesterday, who insists on working with you all day and then just happens to turn up on your doorstep asking you out to the pub, isn't asking you out for a date?" She shook her head. "In my day, that was called a date."

I leave before she can embarrass me even more. Back in my flat, Jack is looking at the meager collection of games.

"Sorry, Mary wanted to chat," I say.

"No worries. I like your games. I used to play *Pro Skater 3* before I left for America. Dad made me leave everything behind when we flew out."

I frown at him as I collect my coat. "He didn't let you take any of your things?"

Jack shook his head. "Nothing. He just ripped me away from everything." He's aiming for a light tone, but I can hear the bitterness in his voice and his shoulders slump.

"I'm so sorry," I say. Without thinking, I reach out and pull him into a hug. There's a moment's startled resistance and then he hugs me back.

We stay like that for a minute, and then he says, "Come on, let's get that beer. After the day I've had, I could do with getting hammered."

I let him go with reluctance. He feels good in my arms.

We head for the Victoria rather than the Angel, although that's closer. Even with my limited knowledge of pubs, I know to avoid the Angel, which is frequently subject to raids from the police for drugs.

The Victoria is off the beaten path, and caters to the locals. I worry I'll stand out, but it turns out Jack knows the landlord.

"Doug is a friend of my mum's... was a friend. He told me to look him up if I was ever around again."

As soon as we walk in, a man behind the bar smiles at us in greeting. I want to run. The noise of people laughing and talking is too much, and it's crowded, but Jack grabs me by the arm and hauls me over to the bar.

"Evening, gentlemen. What can I get you?"

Jack beams at the barman. "Doug, good to see you again." I notice he's using his English accent. When the man smiles at him uncertainly, Jack says, "I'm Harry Cooper, Melanie's son."

"Harry? Christ, I hardly recognised you, son. You're so tall now." Doug pumps his hand enthusiastically, ignoring all the people waving their ten-pound notes.

"Great to see you, Doug."

Doug ignores a man trying to attract his attention. "Your mum would be so proud if she could see you now."

Jack grows quiet and still next to me. "Do you think so?"

He sounds like a little boy seeking approval, and I want to hug him. But that wouldn't be a good idea.

Jack seems to shake off his melancholy and says, "Doug, this is David. He helps at the homeless shelter. David, Doug is the landlord here."

"Pleased to meet you, David."

I shake Doug's meaty hand, trying not to show how freaked I am by people being so freaking *nice* to me. If I'd walked in here three months ago, the landlord would have kicked me out.

"What do you want, David?" Jack asks.

"Uh...." Fuck knows. "Whatever you're having."

He gives me an odd look but nods, ordering two Bud Lights. Doug says the first round is on the house. We both thank him and look around for somewhere to sit. In the far corner is a table with just room for the two of us. Before I can point it out, Jack is weaving his way to the table, cutting off a couple who'd been heading for it. He ignores their glares and waves at me.

I concentrate on not having a panic attack as I join him. The low ceiling and the sheer crush of people are making my heart pound. There is little room, and Jack suggests I sit next to him so the thwarted couple can take the other side. They nod, rather ungratefully, I think, and I press up close to Jack. The feel of his solid body grounds me. He's much bigger than I remember, and I wonder if he plays sport back home.

"Basketball and track," he confirms when I ask. "I didn't have a choice. The school specialises in sports, and I had to do something. At least it wasn't football or cricket."

"You feel... look good," I murmur, and even in the low light I see him blush.

I feel painfully thin and scrawny next to him. The last couple of years have taken a real toll on my body. I can't see why Jack would be interested in someone like me.

"It's good to be back here," he says, stretching out his legs. "I've missed England so much. Marmite. *EastEnders.* Yorkshire pudding."

"Is it hot in North Carolina?" I have no idea where North Carolina is.

"Hotter than here in the summer."

"That must be hard with your pale skin." Then it's my turn to blush—I've just made it obvious I've been watching him.

"Yeah. I stand next to all the tanned jocks and

look like a nerd."

"The cheerleaders aren't interested?" I tease.

Jack hesitates and then shakes his head. "It doesn't matter. It's mutual." He looks at me uncertainly. "I'm not reading this wrong, am I? You are gay?"

I nod. "Yeah."

"Thank fuck for that," he says forcefully.

I laugh and take a swig of my bottle. "Worried you'd read me wrong?"

He looks at me honestly. "I can't read you like I can most boys. The guys around my school are open books. Eat, sports, fuck. That's all they want to do. You seem different. Quieter, closed off."

I nod again. "I guess that's true. I'm not good at being around people."

"Is that because of your illness?"

"Something like that." I hope my tone suggests I don't want to talk about it.

Luckily he takes the hint and changes the subject. To my surprise, he starts talking about his time with "Danny." I realise, in the thirteen months since he left, Jack has not forgotten about Danny at all. I suppose I should find it odd he wants to talk about an ex-boyfriend to another man he's interested in, but Jack is still very young, and I'm guessing still quite inexperienced. He doesn't see anything wrong in what he's doing.

"I wish you'd met him," he says wistfully after he concludes "our" tale.

"He sounds like a nice guy," I say lamely.

"He was."

"Do you still want to see him?"

He looks at me then, maybe hearing an edge to my voice. "No," he says eventually. "I don't think I'll see him again."

I have a decision to make, and it's now or never. Jack will be gone soon, and I can either say good-bye now or maybe get my closure.

"Do you wanna get out of here?" I ask huskily.

Jack swallows. I can see his Adam's apple bob up and down. "Yeah," he says.

We leave, and he waves at Doug as we go. Doug rolls his eyes and makes him promise to return before he goes home.

"Where can we go?" he asks.

That makes me hesitate. I could take him back to my place, but it's something I haven't discussed with Mary and Sylvia. I know Mary had said it was okay for me to bring a boyfriend back but in their eyes I've only just met Jack. I don't know how they would feel about me bringing him back so soon. I need to talk to Mary.

I look at Jack. "I can't bring you back—not yet."

He nods. "I'm the same." He laughs. "Perhaps we should have stayed at the pub."

"We could always find a quiet corner," I suggest.

"The park?"

No, definitely not there. Strangely enough, I don't want to take Jack to the place I had with Harry—even though they're one and the same person.

"I know a place we can go," I say. And I lead him around the streets until we reach the edge of the common. There's a bench by the river that's normally used by couples wanting to make out, and sure enough, it's occupied, but further along the river is another bench. Not many people venture that far along in the dark. I hold out my hand and guide him along the path.

I can't see his expression in the dark, but I can hear his amusement when he asks if we're going far as he didn't bring his night-vision goggles.

"Geek."

"Nothing wrong with being a geek," he counters.

"I thought you were a jock."

"As I said, not by choice."

We reach the bench and sit down. I turn to ask if I can kiss him, and then he's all over me, straddling my thighs on the bench. I have to hang on to him to make sure he doesn't fall off.

Our mouths meet, clumsy and off-centre in the dark, but it doesn't matter. What matters is that for the first time in more than a year, I feel like I'm home again. I wonder if he feels the same way.

Jack pulls back, dragging in air with a shaky breath. "Fuck," he manages. "Fuck."

"No lube," I point out.

"Who cares? Use spit if you have to."

It's tempting, but I'm damned sure his ass is still virgin. I don't know why I'm sure, but I am, and there's no way I'm popping his cherry without plenty of lube.

"Not tonight. I need a bed to fuck in."

"Old man," he teases.

I push my hips up, sliding my dick along his denim-covered ass. I'm hard, and even with the clothing, there's no way he can't feel it. "Old man?"

He doesn't answer immediately. He's busy unzipping my coat and then finding his way under the jumper I'm wearing. His hands are freezing cold.

My shriek echoes in the silence. "Ow. You fucker. Get them off me."

Jack gives a wicked laugh. "A little cold, are they?"

"They're fucking blocks of ice, you fucking bastard."

"Stop swearing," he chides, but he doesn't remove his hands.

Two can play at that game. "I'm sorry," I say sweetly and kiss him again. I make sure my mouth is distracting him as I undo his jeans and wrap my equally cold hand around his cock.

His yell of fury more than rivals mine.

"I'm gonna kill you," he warns.

"No, you're not." Because my now less cold hand is still wrapped around his dick, and despite the momentary flag, the shaft is warm and hard in my grasp. I swipe my thumb over the top, feeling the sticky precome as I smear it over the glans.

Jack whines, thrusting up for more. He's hanging onto my coat with one hand to keep his balance and has the other on my chest, palm flat, grazing my nipple with a nail.

I can't decide if I want to suck him or bring him off in my hand. He decides for me, begging me to let him come. Christ, *let* him come. I could keep him like this for hours, begging for it and on the edge. I forget he's eighteen, desperate, and he shouts as he comes messily all over my hand.

He thunks his head down onto my shoulder as he recovers. I haven't let go of his dick, and to my surprise, it doesn't soften. Instead, within a minute he's moving again, begging softly for more. I can't lift him off, and the bench isn't wide enough for us to both sit and kneel.

"Get off me and sit down," I order, and he does, although he moans when I let go of his dick. Then I'm on my knees, praying there are no needles or other nasty surprises on the ground, and I suck him down to the root. With the edge taken off, I can lick and suck Jack to another tumultuous climax. His prick is heavy in my mouth, and his sac full and tight. He's begging again, soft words I can't quite hear. I hear one word clearly, though, as his shaft hardens impossibly more in my mouth and then fills my mouth with come.

"Danny!"

I swallow and sit up, wiping my mouth with the back of my hand. "David. Not Danny."

"Huh?" His voice is ragged and heavy.

"My name is David."

Jack sits up straight. "Fuck! I'm sorry. I didn't mean.... I know it's you."

I place my hands on his thighs, thickly muscled and a fucking turn-on. "Don't do this with me as a substitute for him, okay?"

"I'm not. Honestly, David, I just...." I feel him squirm. "I just feel the same way about you that I did about him. Really comfortable. Shit! I'm a teenager and I sound like my dad."

I chuckle to relieve the tension. "It's okay. I feel the same way too. Just don't be calling me the wrong name too many times."

"Promise. Now, what about you?"

What about me? Oh. *Oh!* Oh yeah, I could do with a hand. I stand up and take his hand to wrap around my cock.

He leans forward to suck my cock, but I pull away.

"No, don't."

"You don't want me to blow you?" he asks, sounding hurt.

"Not without a rubber. You… uh… you don't know where I've been."

"You didn't use one for me," he points out.

Fuck, this is awkward. "Did I make the wrong decision?" I ask, going on the offensive.

There is silence, and then he says, "No."

"Then jack me off and next time we'll get supplies."

Bringing me off doesn't take long. I close my eyes and feel my orgasm coiling in the pit of my back. His technique is as sloppy and awkward as I remember, but it's *his* hand around my dick, and *his* mouth pressed against my belly. The only sounds are our harsh breaths as I come, spilling over his hand.

I mouth my love's name into the night. He can't hear and he'll never know.

"Harry."

Chapter 13

Boxing Day into December 27, 2003

We part eventually, after the cold threatens frostbite to delicate areas of the body. But not before I press Jack up against a wall and wank him so slowly he is almost crying with need.

He leaves me with a promise of bringing supplies if I clear it with Mary. That's one conversation I'm not looking forward to having. He also leaves me with a hickey on my neck. When I look at it the next morning, I sigh. I don't have any clothes that will cover the dark bruise, and sure enough, as soon as I walk in Mary's kitchen, she fixes her gaze on my neck.

"Good night?" she asks.

I grunt, and pull out the twenty-pound note. "Here, I didn't use it last night."

"Keep it," she says as she pours herself a cup of tea. "You'll probably need it again."

I sit down at the table, and she sits opposite me. I can see the curiosity written all over her face.

"What?" I ask.

"You haven't told me whether it was a good night or not."

"We went to the Victoria," I say.

"I haven't been there in years. My friend Betty goes there every Thursday lunchtime before bingo. Says there's a nice barman there—Doug something or other."

"I met him. He used to be a friend of Jack's mum, and he's the landlord, not just the barman."

"Then what did you do? You got in so late."

I'm not fooled by the innocent expression on her face. The woman wants to know what we did and she means to find out.

"We went down by the river." I say.

She looks at my neck again. "I can see he was busy."

I look at her steadily. "I didn't fuck him for money." I'm gratified by the horrified expression on her face.

"I didn't think you had," she exclaims.

"Didn't you?"

"No!"

"You thought about it, though."

She sighs and nods. "It's happened before. A couple of the girls tried to conduct their *business* out of here. I asked them to leave when they didn't stop." She smiles at me. "But you and Jack have history, don't you?"

"Yeah."

"Yes," Mary says primly. "Tell me about it?"

It's a suggestion, not an order. I bite my lip. "You probably know most of it. Danny met Harry, in the park, about eighteen months ago."

She grins. "It sounds like that film—what was it?"

I frown. "Film?"

"I know it. It's on the tip of my tongue." Mary clicks her fingers. "*When Harry Met Sally*! That's it! Lovely film. Meg Ryan was very cute, and I've always liked Billy Crystal."

At my puzzled expression, she sighs. "I guess it's another one before your time. Anyway, you met him in the park. Were you living there then?"

I nod. "Yeah... yes. Harry was one of the kids that walked through the park on the way to school. He was being bullied by the other kids. I had no idea he was having problems." I'm ashamed of that. Ashamed to admit I'd let a kid suffer because I avoided Joe and George.

Mary reaches over to squeeze my hand. "I understand. The kids probably gave you a hard time as well?"

"Some did. Most didn't even know I was there. I was very good at being invisible."

"So what happened?"

"I saw two of the kids beat him up and went to stop it. One of them had a knife."

Mary looked at me when I didn't say anymore. "He was very lucky you were there. What happened then?"

"Nothing, really. Harry was more pissed that I'd interfered, in case the boys went after him again. Then he came to find me a couple of days later with a McDonald's as a thank-you."

"There isn't a McDonald's in town."

"I know. He had his mum drive to Guildford to get one."

"Why did he do that?"

"Because I told him to bring me a McDonald's

next time he was in the park."

She smiles. "You should have asked for a pizza."

I shake my head. "I don't like pizza that much."

"Then what happened?" Mary gets up to pour herself some more tea, and then sits down to hear my answer.

I look at her steadily. "You have a lot of questions."

"You don't have to answer them," she points out.

That's true, but she knows I'm going to anyway. "He kept coming back. Usually with food. I told him to leave me alone, but he wouldn't."

"Did anything else happen?" Her expression made it clear what she meant.

"Sort of. Not much. He was sixteen."

"You were only eighteen."

"And homeless."

"But something happened?"

"He told me he was gay. Like I hadn't worked that out for myself. He asked me to kiss him. I refused."

"Why? Didn't you like him?"

"I was skanky. I didn't bathe or clean my teeth. I wasn't going to let his first kiss be from someone like me."

"What did he say?"

"He brought me a toothbrush, toothpaste, and mouthwash."

Mary burst out laughing. "Now I've met Jack, I can see him doing that."

I gave her a wry smile. "Yeah, it's just the sort of

thing he'd do."

"So?"

"So I cleaned up and gave him his first kiss."

"Was it good?"

"None of your business," I say easily.

"I suppose not," she admits. "Is that all?"

"No, but we didn't do much more." I wasn't going to tell her what we *did* do. "I got to meet his mum, and Harry insisted on looking after me. Then one day he wasn't there anymore. No more food, no more kisses, nothing else until two days ago, when he returned as Jack looking for Danny."

"And you are David."

"I am David."

"You should tell him."

"No." A flat-out no. It isn't up for discussion.

"Hmmm." She makes that noise that tells me she thinks I'm being an idiot.

"You don't understand. Danny is dead. David doesn't come with history. He's not damaged goods. Jack will only be around for another few days, and then I'll never see him again. Let me be David."

Mary nods slowly. "If you're sure that's what you want. He's still looking for Danny. Aren't you just a stand-in?"

"Danny's dead. He'll have fun, and so will I."

"Which leads me to the next question. Where were you last night? It was freezing and you were out for hours."

"By the river."

"Danny... David," she amends at my glare. "You can't afford to get cold after having pneumonia.

Why didn't you come back here?"

"Well, because we hadn't discussed it, and I was worried about what you'd say," I say, flustered by her direct approach. God knows why, the two women are nothing if not direct.

"You bring him back here. Thank you for thinking of me, but you need to keep warm."

"What about sex?" Two can play at being blunt.

"I'm a bit old for a threesome, dear."

"Mary!" My cheeks heat up. She wins.

She rolls her eyes. "I'm not stupid, David. I know you'll be having sex. Just be careful, okay?"

"Harry's going to bring supplies." *Please, God, don't ask me what that entails.*

"That's good, but you should get your own."

I blush even harder. "I don't have any money. I need to sort out my benefits."

"You've got the twenty-pound note," she pointed out.

"Oh yes. Is anywhere open today?"

"It's a Saturday. Most places will be open."

"I'll go into town." I look at the woman who has transformed my life. "Thank you, Mary. I'll never be able to thank you enough for everything you have done for me."

She looks pleased. "Get over with you. I'm just glad I'm in a position to help. Thank Sylvia if you have to thank anyone. She's the one who mentioned you."

I lean forward and place my hand over hers. "It's more than just the home. It's the care and affection you've given me. More than I've had in years from anyone, apart from Harry."

"You are more than welcome, dear, although I shouldn't need to point out Ben tried to help you before. Now get your coat on. I need to go into town as well."

Jack turns up again that evening. I'm tired and crashed out on the sofa, watching a film. He gives me a grin at the suggestion we spend the night in, and joins me on the sofa, close but not too close. By the end of the film, I've got my head on his chest. I'm pretty sure I dozed off partway through, but I wake up for the end explosions. Nearly all of Mary's films seem to involve explosions.

"Hey."

I look up to see Jack smiling at me. He looks so young, but Harry's innocence is gone, ripped away by the death of his mother, I suppose.

"Kiss me," I say, and he bends down to place his lips on mine. It's awkward at first, and then we wriggle to get the angle just right, and the kissing is wet, and hot. He explores my mouth, demanding that I open up to him. Virginal he might be, but Jack knows what he wants, and at the moment, he wants me. I'm not objecting.

I slide a hand under his jumper to feel his warm skin. Jack moans against my open mouth. His nipples are hard against my fingertips, and he shivers every time I press down on them. He's really responsive to every move I make, and it makes me even harder. I sit up so I can lean over him. I want to push him down into the sofa cushions and explore every part of him. The last time I had the luxury of being with someone was the awkward fumbling with Harry. Since then, it's been blow jobs and taking it up the arse for cold hard cash. No intimacy or affection, no time to get to know a body. Not that I'd have wanted to get to know the men who paid me. But that was then and this is now.

Jack tries to sit up, but I keep him pinned to the sofa. "Take me to bed," he begs.

It occurs to me that locking the door from the house might be a good idea before we fuck. I don't even know if the door has a lock.

"Hold that thought," I say, and I head for the door, ignoring Jack's pout. Thankfully there is a key in the lock, and within seconds I'm back and helping Jack off the sofa. Jack immediately sinks to his knees and pulls down my joggers and boxers.

"I thought you wanted me to take you to bed?" I say, although since his intention is obvious, I'm not that bothered.

Jack looks up and licks his lips. Fuck, if that doesn't make me grow harder. From the harsh intake of breath, Jack sees my reaction.

"Have you done this before?" I ask, curious to see what he says.

He hesitates, and I can almost see him think about lying to me, then he shakes his head. "Not since Danny. I've had it done to me a few times."

It's on the tip of my tongue to ask who the other men were.

"He was my first. And a couple of the guys from school sucked me off, but I've never done it to anyone else."

"Why not?" I ask, tangling my fingers in his hair.

He hesitates again. "I promised myself I would find Danny."

I still my fingers in his hair. "I'm not Danny."

"I know. But they told me Danny died." *They did?* "I know I'll never see Danny again, and I want you so bad."

Who are they? I needed to ask more questions but not now.

"I want you too." I fumble in my pocket and hand him a foil packet.

Jack pulls a face, but obediently rolls the condom down my cock. He's more skilled than he was last year despite not having much practice, I notice, and I can't deny how jealous that makes me. He leans forward to touch my dick with his tongue. I jerk at the first touch of him. He pulls away as if he's done something wrong, but I guide him back. "More. That's good."

He looks up, unsure.

"Do whatever you want," I say, encouraging him with gentle pressure.

He huffs out a breath and leans forward again, his tongue coming out to explore the head of my cock. I hold my breath, almost too scared to breathe in case it frightens him away again. But he makes this noise, half moan, half grunt, as he holds on to my hips, digging his fingers into them, and then he's truly licking and sucking me, and it's all I can do to keep on my feet.

It's clumsy and he grazes my skin too often

with his teeth, but he's into it, into me, and I don't fucking care. We can improve the technique later. I ignore the fact there isn't going to be a later.

I'm going to come and I don't want that. I want to come buried in his arse. He glares at me as I tug on his hair.

"Want to take you to bed," I say, and I hold out my hand.

He nods, wiping his mouth with the back of his hand, and gets unsteadily to his feet. "Want you too."

Holding up my joggers as best as I can, I dispose of the condom and shuffle over to the bed and turn to Jack. Undressing him takes a long time. I want to explore his body. He's big. I know I thought that before, but with the two of us standing together, it's obvious he has far outstripped me in development—in all areas.

Once again I feel inadequate, but Jack doesn't seem to care. He traces a path over my neck with one fingertip. "You're gorgeous," he says.

I look away. "Don't give me that. I'm too skinny."

To my surprise, he agrees. "You are. I can see every rib, but you've been ill. You're still gorgeous."

"You need your eyes checked."

He steps into my space. "I can see just fine. Old people like you need their eyes checked."

"Cheeky git." I slap his arse, the sound ringing out into the quiet room.

Apart from a sharply indrawn breath, he doesn't make any objection, but I apologise anyway.

"I liked it," he whispers.

I swallow hard. Fuck, if we just had more time.

"What happened here?" he asks, tracing the pink scar left by the knife.

"Got stabbed."

"Fuck. When was that?"

"Last year," I say shortly, not wanting to give away too much information.

"What...?"

"Do you want to talk or fuck?" I ask, cutting him off.

He looks at me, his eyes huge. "Just tell me they got the bastard that hurt you."

I nod. George was caught and put away. Joe got community service. If it had been just me as a witness, the courts might have accepted their defence of the homeless guy assaulting them, but an elderly couple witnessed the stabbing and saw them running away.

I hope the bastards rot.

"Good," he says. "Now fuck me."

"Get on the bed."

"Wait, we need lube and condoms. They're in my coat pocket."

"I bought some today. In the bedside table."

At Jack's inquiring look, I say, "Part of my conversation with Mary. She gave me the money to be safe."

He crows as I blush. "I'd love to have been a fly on the wall for that conversation."

"Ha-ha," I say sourly.

"You're very lucky. I can't imagine having that

conversation with my dad, let alone my gran."

"Me neither. Mary is one of a kind."

"What about your parents?"

"Are we going to fuck or are we going to exchange parental stories?" I ask quickly.

"We're going to fuck like bunnies," Jack assures me.

Glad he's easily diverted, I push him onto the bed. "Let the bunny-fucking commence."

Jack spreads his legs, and my mouth goes dry at the sight of him spread open like that. I want to take him now, push him down into the sheets and fuck him hard, but this is his first time, and no way is it going to be like my fucks. Memories of being cold, and the pain from my face being pushed against a brick wall, rancid sweat, and being held so I couldn't get away flood my mind. I force them away. They have no place here, with us.

I kneel on the bed between his legs and reach for the lube. Jack looks very young and uncertain as he watches me, his bottom lip caught between his teeth. He wants this, it's obvious, but he's nervous.

"Tell me if I hurt you." I lean over him and slide one slick finger between his arse cheeks. He closes his eyes as I press in. "Open your eyes," I say, needing that contact with him. He opens his eyes slowly, almost reluctantly, it seems. "Are you okay?"

Jack nods. "Feels odd."

"I can stop." *Please, please, don't make me stop.*

"Don't you dare," he says, almost savagely,

reaching out to clamp around my wrist. His hand is sweaty and slips on my skin, but he holds on as tight as he can.

"I won't." It's a promise. A vow.

When I think Jack's ready, I insert another finger. I revel in being allowed to take the time to make it right. By the time he is humping the air, desperate for more, I'm more than ready too. I ease my sheathed cock into his tight channel. Fuck, he's so tight, but he's doing his best to open for me. I go slowly, and by the time I'm seated, Jack is panting hard, sweat beading across his brow.

"Okay?" I ask, my voice almost too loud in the stillness of the room. I wish I'd left the TV on.

"Yeah." Jack gives me a smile. "You gotta move or I'm going to pop before we get started."

I laugh in relief, but his cock is hard, flushed angry red and weeping from the tip. "Hold on just a bit longer."

"You're fucking joking, aren't you?"

I pull out, and he gasps. "Hold on," I order again and push back in. My rhythm is ragged, but I thrust into him, reveling in his gasps and pleas. I'm leaning over him, feeling his cock slap against our bellies.

"David! David. Gotta...." He comes, his body clamping down on mine so tight it holds back my own orgasm. When I do climax, it's almost painful in its intensity.

"Fuck!" I yell, forgetting I could be heard elsewhere. All I can think about is the relief of my balls emptying into the condom, and the hard, sharp pants of the boy underneath me.

"Breathe out," I say as I pull out, making sure I hold on to the condom.

Jack does as he's told, but I can see him wince as I withdraw. I get rid of the condom and lie on the bed next to him, stroking his torso as we both calm down. Slowly the flush leaves his skin, and his breathing returns to normal.

"That was fucking amazing," he whispers.

"Are you sure? You don't hurt too much?" I've never cared about any of my past "partners," except for Steve and Harry, but I want to make sure Jack is okay.

"I feel like someone stuck a two-by-four up my arse, but it was fucking amazing." Jack raises himself on one elbow as he turns to face me. "David, I'm glad it was you."

David, not Danny.

"I'm glad it was you," I respond.

He leans forward to kiss me. I haven't done much kissing before. No one's wanted to kiss me since Harry left. Jack doesn't kiss like Harry. Harry was soft and unsure. Jack kisses like he means it. I appreciate the difference.

I also appreciate the way he's now kissing down my abs, along the thin line of hair. "You got something on your mind?" I ask, raising one eyebrow as he looks at me.

"Yeah." Jack gives me a wicked smirk.

"What's that?"

He rises up over me and reaches for the rubbers. He's hard again. "I'm going to fuck you now."

I can do that.

Chapter 14

December 27

Sylvia knocks on my door later that evening. It's almost eleven and I'm lying on the wreck of the bed. Jack left earlier with more kisses and apologies that he had to see his grandma. I don't mind. It gives me time to think. I need to be able to separate myself from the relationship that's developing. Jack tells me he's flying back on the fourth of January. That means I have him for eight more days, less if you count the last day and New Year's Eve and Day. We haven't had that discussion yet.

"Hello," I yell when Sylvia doesn't come in.

"The door's locked." She doesn't sound pleased.

"Oh, sorry." I jump out of bed and run to open the door.

Sylvia's leaning against the doorframe, a disgruntled look on her face.

"Are you okay?" I ask.

"I don't know. You tell me," she says.

I stand back and beckon her into the room. She sniffs the air, and her frown deepens even more. I can tell what she smells. The scent of spunk and sweat is heavy.

"You've had someone here," she says.

I nod. "Jack."

"Jack? From the shelter?"

"Yeah. We went out for a drink last night, and then he came round here today. Is that a problem?" I know my voice is sharp, but I'm not sure why she's bitching.

"You think it's acceptable to bring men back here to my mother's home?" She scowls at me.

I stare at her for a moment. "You think I'm charging Jack to fuck?"

"I didn't say that."

"That's what you meant, though, isn't it?"

She coughs and looks away.

"Be honest. I have a friend back and the first thing you think of is that I'm hustling him."

"I... well, are you?" she asks, going on the offensive.

I shake my head. "I haven't broken any of your mother's rules. If you don't believe me, ask Mary." I can see she doesn't look convinced. "Look, it's too late now. I'll leave in the morning."

"I'm not kicking you out," Sylvia says quickly.

"You don't trust me. Thanks for letting me stay whilst I was ill, but I'm not staying where I'm not wanted. Now, if that's all...?" I fold my arms and make it clear she's not welcome anymore.

"I do trust you," she says as I herd her out of the room.

"No, you don't. Good night." I shut the door in her face and deliberately lock it.

I climb back into bed and stare up at the ceiling. Once again I'm facing eviction, and this time I curse myself for letting my guard down. The clock on the bedside table projects onto the ceiling. The minutes pass slowly. At 3:00 a.m. I give up trying to sleep and get up to make myself a hot chocolate.

I curl up on the sofa, appreciating the comfort as I sip at the hot drink, not bothering to wait for it to cool down. If I'm going to be sleeping out tomorrow night, I need to find some cardboard and a sleeping bag. It's bloody cold, so I'll need blankets as well. I make a plan to head for the shelter in the morning to see what they have.

The knock at the door wakes me up from a light doze. I almost call out for whoever it is to come in, but then I remember I locked the door. I'm not surprised to see Sylvia, but Mary is with her as well. Judging from the tiredness in their faces, neither woman has been to bed.

"Please, may we come in?" Mary asks. "We saw the light on."

I look over my shoulder at the clock on the wall. It's four thirty. "Do you want me to go now?"

Mary pushed in front of Sylvia. "Don't talk rubbish. We don't want you to go at all. We didn't spend all those weeks nursing you only to throw you out on a misunderstanding."

"Misunderstanding?" I look at Sylvia as I say it.

She looks embarrassed. "I didn't realise you'd spoken to Mum already. You didn't tell me that."

"You didn't ask," I say coldly. "You just assumed I was fucking for cash."

"I didn't *say* that," Sylvia says.

"Neither of us said that," Mary says. She sounds

weary. "You jumped in with that idea before we'd even started." I open my mouth to argue, but she continues, "Look, come and have a drink with us. We're all tired, but none of us can sleep until we've sorted it out."

"I'll find a top." I reach for the hoodie I wore yesterday, and then follow them into the kitchen.

Mary puts on the kettle and opens the cupboard. "Tea?" she asks over her shoulder. Sylvia says yes and so do I. I don't like tea, but the two women drink so much it's easier to say yes.

I drink my tea, trying not to pull a face. I wish I'd asked for another hot chocolate. I wait for one of them to start talking. They wanted the council of war, they can talk first.

Sylvia clears her throat. "I'm sorry, Danny... David. I was wrong to accuse you of anything before I spoke to Mum. She said she'd already told you to bring Jack back here."

I stare at her steadily, because if I speak, I'm going to say something I'll regret.

She looks at me as if she expects a reply, and then she sighs. "I won't make that mistake again."

"She was just protecting me," Mary says. "You know we've had problems with other kids in the past."

They both seem to be waiting for a response. You know what? I don't care. Fuck them both.

"I'm going to bed," I announce, and I leave the room.

"David, come back here." Mary sounds annoyed now.

I close the door. I'll talk to them after I've had

some sleep. I'm exhausted and drained, and the thrill of making love to Jack has been totally lost in the emotional battering that followed. I crawl into bed and bury my nose in the smell of the two of us. I'm convinced I won't be able to sleep but exhaustion wins out and I'm dead to the world before I have time to think.

December 28

Banging on two doors wakes me from a dreamless slumber. Squinting at the clock, I see it's nearly two in the afternoon. The banging continues. I stumble out of bed, and then hesitate, unable to decide which door to head to first.

In the end, I open the house door first, ignore Sylvia, who's waiting there, and jog over to the front door. Jack, I smile at. *He* hasn't upset me.

"Hi." He gives me a grin and leans forward to kiss me. "Have you forgotten we were meeting for lunch?"

Forgotten? Um, yeah. I don't remember the conversation at all. Sex yes, plans no.

Jack looks over my shoulder. "I think Sylvia is waiting to talk to you."

I turn around to see Sylvia still standing by the door, her expression a mixture of pissed and uncomfortable. It's not a good look.

"Did you want to talk to me?" I ask.

Jack obviously picks up on my tone because he looks between the two of us, curiosity on his face.

"We didn't finish our conversation," she says

snippily.

"You got it wrong, you apologised. What else is there to say?" I'm being a dick, and I know it, but I haven't forgiven her for automatically thinking the worst.

"I'll come back later," she snaps. "I hope by then you'll have remembered your manners." She leaves the flat, slamming the door behind her.

I turn to Jack, who's staring at me in amazement. "Sorry about that," I say weakly.

He comes into the flat, closing the door behind him. "What the fuck was that about?"

"Nothing."

"It doesn't sound like nothing," he points out.

I scrub my hand through my hair. "Just a misunderstanding."

He gives me a look, "Uh-huh," and he heads for the kettle. "I'm going to make us a drink. Go and have a shower, then we'll talk."

"What about lunch?"

"We'll go out later. Shower now."

He shoves me, not gently, in the direction of the bathroom. I think about arguing but decide I don't want to piss off someone else today. Despite my attitude, I don't like upsetting people. My dad used to do it all the time, and I swore I wouldn't be like that bastard.

I don't rush in the shower, and when I walk out of the bathroom, a towel wrapped around my waist, Jack is eating a croissant and reading the *Daily Mail*.

"You've been to see Mary." *I sound accusing... deep breath... I need to chill.*

Jack looks up from the newspaper. "Yep. You've been a prat, haven't you?"

I think about arguing but I'm too tired. "Yeah."

"Here, eat something. Then you can tell me what happened." He pats the sofa next to him. Thankfully, he puts the paper down.

"I'm surprised Mary hasn't told you," I say sourly.

"Well, she did. But I want to hear it from your own lips." To emphasise the point, he stares at my mouth.

I know I'm going red. "Don't do that."

"Sorry," he says totally insincerely.

"Tell me what happened." This time his tone is gentle.

I take a deep breath. "Sylvia accused me of bringing you back here and charging you for sex."

He nods. "And then?"

I frown at him. "You don't seem surprised."

"They told me this. They also said none of you slept. Then, when Sylvia tried to apologise, you told her to eff off."

"I did no such thing."

"You walked out after she said she was sorry."

I hate the voice of reason. "She made me angry. They both did. I thought they knew me better than that." I pick at the croissant Jack gives me. "I promised them I'd never hustle here, and the first time I bring a boy back, they don't believe me."

"They do believe you, but it's not like it hasn't happened before."

"I haven't done it before."

"Dipshit. I meant other kids. They told me that,

as well."

I give him a look. "You seem to have had quite a conversation for the ten minutes I was in the shower."

Unfazed, Jack smiles at me. "They're worried and pissed."

"Yeah, I get that. I thought they were going to throw me out." I look away, not wanting him to see how vulnerable I am, how fucking hurt by their accusations. *I'm David*, I keep telling myself. *David, not Danny*. Of course, it fools no one.

He hugs me tight. "Fucking idiot. Why would they do that? Now eat that croissant."

"I'm not hungry."

"Eat!"

Jesus, for a kid he's fucking bossy. I eat.

The shredded croissant and the orange juice he shoved in my hand gurgle in my stomach unhappily. I'm not convinced that I'm not going to barf. Keeping my eyes closed seems to help, and I sit very still.

"David?"

I open my eyes to see Sylvia standing in front of me.

"Third time lucky?" she says hopefully.

Ignoring the lurch in my gut, I stand up and step into her open arms. "I'm sorry," I manage as I press my cheek against her hair.

Sylvia squeezes me hard. "You don't have to be sorry for anything. You weren't the idiot."

"Yeah, I was. I'm just so scared." Then I shut up, because Jack is in the room, but I'm still not secure enough to step away from her.

"You've kissed and made up, then?" Mary says.

I look up see Mary and Ben standing next to Jack. "What's this? An intervention?"

Ben nodded. "It was, but you seem to be doing fine without it."

I sigh as Sylvia squeezes me tight. She stands back and wipes her eyes. "Do you want a cuppa?"

I pull a face. "Do I have to drink tea?"

"A Coke. Just this once." Sylvia looks over at Mary. "What do you think? Does he deserve fizzy?"

Mary huffs. "Just this time."

I roll my eyes at them. "I'm twenty years old. I think I've got past the age of worrying about my teeth."

"You think it stops because you're so old?" Sylvia laughs at me, and Ben joins in. "Mum still reminds me to clean my teeth every night."

"You don't!" I gape at Mary.

"Good dental hygiene is important," Mary says primly. "Fizzy rots your teeth."

"Jack, do you want a Coke?"

"Can I have a cup of coffee, please?"

From the look on Mary's face, Jack could have asked for hemlock. "Coffee? I think we might have a jar somewhere."

"For heaven's sake, you know we have coffee." Sylvia grinned at Jack. "Mum's a real snob about coffee."

"I'm not a snob. I just think coffee is revolting."

"I don't like coffee either," I confide to Mary. "Mum used to make coffee with chicory in, and it put me off for life."

Jack's looking at me curiously, and I curse myself for mentioning my mum. Thankfully Mary grins at me and talks before Jack can ask questions.

"Coke, coffee, and three teas coming up. Ben, can you look at the oven? It's making some really odd noises."

"Mum, we didn't get Ben over here to make him work," Sylvia chides.

Ben shakes his head. "It's no problem. I'm happy to help. But you should have asked Da… David. He's really good at DIY." He grins at Sylvia and holds his arm out for Mary.

Mary nods at me. "Perhaps you can be trusted with power tools."

And then another piece of the puzzle falls into place as the memories of a long-ago conversation I'd had with Ben about the woman he has loved forever bubbles to the surface.

"Oh. Ben. You idiot," I mutter as they leave the room.

"Huh?" Jack looks confused.

"No worries. I'll explain later. Better get into the kitchen before Mary gets pissed at us both."

"Okay." Jack presses a kiss to my lips, which turns into another kiss, and maybe some groping before we actually leave my flat.

The three adults are sitting around the kitchen table when I walk in, Jack hard on my heels.

Mary looks up. "I thought we were going to have to send out a search party. What kept you?"

"Shh, Mum, they were busy." Sylvia throws a grin at me.

"Busy," I agree. I wonder how I could have missed Ben's soppy expression before when he looks at Sylvia. Ben sees me watching him and blushes as I flick my gaze to Sylvia. Oh boy, I can't wait to have *that* conversation.

Jack moves his chair close to mine as we sit down. It doesn't seem to bother him to be so openly gay in front of the other three. I realise it does bother me. I can't help expecting them to turn on me in disgust. But of course Ben doesn't turn a hair, and I realise how damn stupid I am expecting Mary and Sylvia to, in light of what happened to Allan. Tentatively, I take Jack's hand in mine, and promptly four people beam at me. I want to crawl under a rock and hide from all the attention. But Jack holds my hand so tightly I stay where I am, trying hard to keep a smile on my face.

After the drink, Jack wants to go out. He has plans but he doesn't seem to want to talk about them. He asks Ben if he would mind giving us a lift on his way back to the shelter.

When we end up at the crematorium, I understand why he's so cagey. Jack wants to visit his mum but he doesn't know how to ask me to go with him.

He looks at me with a pleading expression as we stand at the gates. Ben offers to wait for us, but I say we'll get the bus back. I don't want Jack to feel he has to rush.

"We buried her ashes under a rose bush before

we left for America," he says. "I wanted a proper burial and so did she, but Dad wouldn't pay for it."

"Do you remember where it is?"

"The Garden of Remembrance is over there." Jack points to a large garden set back from the path. "I don't remember exactly which path, but I know there was a stone dog nearby."

I hold out my hand to him. "Come on then. There can't be too many stone dogs to find."

After the fifteenth stone dog, I'm beginning to lose hope. "Are you sure it was a dog?"

The light is fading and the crematorium is going to close in half an hour. I watch Jack looking around in despair, and then out of the corner of my eye, I see a small sign that says *Melanie Cooper 14.6.57-17.11.2002. Beloved mother of Jonathan Cooper.*

"I've found it, Jack. Look!" I drag him over to the small rosebush, little more than a cut-down stump now.

The relief on his face brings a lump to my throat, as does the way he traces the lettering on the sign.

I stand back to give him a moment with his mum. I can't deny I'm jealous of the relationship Jack must have had with his mum. My mother had been friendly enough, but I was never that close to her. Ironically, I was closer to my dad, which made the fact he threw me out even more tragic. Jack didn't seem that bothered about his dad. He'd lost the one parent he really cared about.

"The crem is closing, boys."

A gruff male voice interrupts my thoughts. I

look up to see a black guy in an old duffel coat and shabby black trousers waving at us from the gate.

"Thanks," I say and look at Jack. "We have to go."

"I know. I should have brought flowers." He gets to his feet and brushes down the knees of his jeans.

"We could come back tomorrow with some," I suggest.

He nods. "Yeah, maybe."

The dude at the gate coughs impatiently. I resist the urge to glare at him. "We're coming. Just give us a moment."

I put my arm around Jack's shoulders as we walk away. The man doesn't give us a second look. I guess people holding each other is common in this place.

"Where do you want to go?" Jack asks as we reach the outer gates.

"Let's get drunk," I say. "I haven't had the chance to do that before."

The gates clang behind us as Jack looks at me speculatively. "You want to get drunk on cheap booze and have a hangover tomorrow?"

I nod. "That sounds like a hell of a good idea."

"Don't say I didn't warn you," he says as we head towards the bus stop.

"Warn me of what?"

Chapter 15

December 29

"I'm dying." I retch miserably into the toilet, feeling the strain in my poor stomach muscles.

"I did warn you," Jack says. He doesn't make a move to help me since he says if he lifts a finger he's going to hurl again.

I think this is unfair. "You didn't tell me I was going to die from a couple of drinks."

"A couple? More like eight. For a guy who's never drunk before, you sure can down 'em."

"You made me drink them. And you didn't tell me what I was drinking."

The previous night, Jack introduced me to snakebite and black. Equal parts lager and cider, and add a dash of black currant. Smooth going down and vile coming back up. As I said, I'm dying. I complain loudly again. Jack is unsympathetic.

"Shut up. You love me."

I freeze. I must look a complete idiot wrapped around the john, unable to move, to speak, because, yeah, I think I do love him. Hell, I've loved this kid since the minute I saved his sorry arse from getting knifed by that psycho. But Jack doesn't know that, and it's way too soon to be declaring undying love for a guy I met four days ago.

"I love you too," Jack says unhelpfully, when my god-awful brain doesn't catch up.

"No, you don't." That's about as much as I can manage.

"Yes, I do. I know we've only just met, but you're amazing, and I'm in love with you."

"You're eighteen years old. You fall in love every five minutes." Christ, could I sound more patronising?

"Says the twenty-year-old," he shoots back.

Okay, I deserve that. "Jack, you're going home in five days. You've got all the hot guys there. What do you want with me?"

I hear a thump, and a minute later he's wrapped his long arms around me and I feel home.

"Don't you believe in love at first sight, David?" he says.

I shake my head. "No," I lie.

"Liar."

"No, I'm not."

He chuckles, his breath brushing my cheek. It smells of toothpaste and the underlying sour/sweet smell of snakebite and vomit. It isn't pleasant, but I don't want him to move. "You'd be more convincing if you weren't hanging on to me so tightly." He doesn't let me go even when I shift in his arms. Once again, I'm reminded just how big the kid is. "I'm in love with a skinny older guy with dark secrets, who needs to trust someone."

I sigh and try to pull away again. "I don't trust anyone."

"I can see that. You can trust me."

"No, I can't, Jack." I turn in his arms, trying not to breathe over him. I haven't had the benefit of having brushed my teeth yet. "You'll go home and I'll be on my own again. You don't know me, you don't know what's going on here."

"Because you won't tell me," he points out. "It's all secrets with you, David."

"You don't understand."

"No, I don't. I'm just some stupid kid."

Fuck. David wasn't meant to come with issues. Danny had the issues. David is a clean slate. No issues—sure.

"I...."

"It doesn't matter, David."

Jack pulls away from me, and we sit on the tiled floor staring at each other. My mouth feels like someone died in it, and so does my head.

"It does matter," I say, determined he see that. "I've got... trust issues... but I love you, Jack Cooper." I give a shaky laugh. "We're sitting on the floor of my bathroom, stinking of puke, and we're having a relationship conversation. Christ, I thought girls wanted these moments, not blokes."

"Are you calling me a girl?" Jack pretends to be outraged, but I can see the relief shining in his eyes.

"You... are... a... girl," I say, grinning at him.

He growls at me and goes to wrestle me to the floor, but I fend him off.

"Uh-uh. Not 'til I've cleaned my teeth. My

mouth tastes fucking horrible."

In less than a week this boy will leave me, but until then I'm going to make the most of our time together.

With a loud groan, Jack rolls over and grins wearily at me. He grumbles as he ends up in the wet patch, but I don't pay any attention. I'm more interested in the state of him. He's a wreck. His dark hair's plastered to his forehead and there are bruises on his hips. I feel smug. I put those marks there and I'm proud of them. I lean forward and lick the dark marks, smiling against his hipbone as I feel his cock twitch.

"You like that, don't you?" he says softly, carding his fingers through my hair.

I nod, not bothering to pretend I don't know what he's talking about. I do like it. I love knowing for these few days he is mine. That each and every mark on his body was put there by me. I licked him, and bit him, and pressed bruises into his skin—and he loved it. With Steve, he was the leader, and I'd followed willingly. But Jack likes to be guided, likes to be held down and fucked. Maybe we're too young to play these games, but we don't have time to wait for our relationship to develop. In a few days, he will be gone, and I will be alone. In the meantime, I'm going to fuck him until he can barely walk.

"How's your head?" he asks.

"I'm dealing. Yours?" Hours of loving later, I barely remember my hangover.

"Same. Listen, my dad is holding a New Year's Eve party. You're invited," Jack says, as I stop marking my territory and lay on his belly, listening to it gurgle under my ear.

"No, thanks." My reaction is so fierce I can't soften the blow.

Jack stops caressing my scalp. "David? More secrets?" he asks, and I can hear the hurt in his voice.

I close my eyes, hoping to drown out the kaleidoscope of images. Steve kissing me. Dad yelling at me, and Mum's face, disappointed and fearful as I'm thrown out of the house. "Don't ask me to explain, Jack. I can't go to your party."

"What are you going to do instead?"

Sleep. Hide. Pretend it's just another night. "Nothing much. I just don't like New Year that much. Can't see the point of a party."

"I'd have thought being with me and celebrating the New Year together was enough?"

I sit up, hiding my face from him. "I can't, Jack."

He puts his hand on my shoulder and the gentle touch almost undoes me. I'm so fucking *weak* now. "Another one of those things you won't talk about?" At my nod I hear him sigh, but he wraps himself around me, enveloping me in his strong arms. "I've got to go. Dad will be pissed if I don't turn up."

"That's cool." I don't want him watching me with those all-knowing eyes. Jack is little more than a boy but he has an old soul, and he makes me want to break down and tell him everything.

"I'll come round as soon as I can," he says.

It's my turn to sigh. I press back into his warmth, feeling his chest hair tickle my back. "I'm sorry, Jack." I feel I'm letting him down.

"You don't have to feel guilty, prat." He holds me tighter. "I just wish you trusted me enough to tell me some of your secrets. You're only twenty. You should be out every night, shagging the girls and boasting about the size of your dick." He laughs at my noise of disgust.

"Firstly, I'd be boasting about shagging the lads, and secondly, your dick is bigger than mine."

"True," he says smugly, "but yours fits my hand," and he demonstrates. He's right. My dick fits snugly into his large hand, and judging from the way it's hardening, my cock is not at all unhappy to be there.

"You think you're so funny, don't you?" I say, blushing at the way my body automatically thrusts into his hand.

"I don't think. I know."

I don't care what he does after that, as he's biting down on my neck and slowly wanking me. What did I say about me leading him? This time he's in control. Perhaps he's trying to make a point.

His hard cock is hot and sticky against my spine. My balls are tight and so sensitive, the brush of his knuckles as he jacks my cock heightening their sensitivity. I come over his fingers as he thumbs the head of my dick. I'm left shaking in his arms, too far gone to help as he rubs himself against my back to climax.

We fall asleep, sticky and sweaty, happy to be together.

Have you ever waited for it all to fall apart? Known that every time you find some happiness it all goes tits up? I was waiting. Sylvia's meltdown, the fact I wouldn't go to the party with Jack, keeping that big-arsed secret... all these things were signs it wasn't going to last. I didn't care, either. I made love—oh, yeah, I'd started to call it making love in my head—to Jack, cooked with Mary, even went back and helped at the shelter with Jack in the run up to New Year, because I just knew the second Big Ben chimed the last fucking bell, the whole being-happy thing would end.

But I'm getting ahead of myself. Before that, we found more time to be sticky and happy.

On the thirtieth, Jack had some family thing to go to. He invited me but I was tired when I woke up, and there was a pain in my chest Sylvia wasn't happy with, so she forced me off to the doctors. It was that or she threatened to manhandle me into A&E. There was no appointment available at my new surgery, so she asked Ben to get the shelter doctor to look at me.

Dr Roberts knows me and my history, and greets me warmly when he arrives.

"Danny, good to see you. After the last time, I wasn't sure I'd see you upon your feet again."

I look up from the reading Ben had shoved in

my hand. He'd put me in the office with some sixth-form prospectuses "to keep you occupied." Jesus, they could be so obvious. "Nor me, doc. Sorry you got dragged in here again. Sylvia is fussing."

The doctor, a good-looking guy with twinkling green eyes and lips to die for—yeah, I thought he was hot—grinned at me. "No choice, huh?"

"You got it. I don't think they've ever given me a choice."

"Take off your shirt and let's listen to your lungs."

He fusses around me for a moment, listening to my chest and then looking down my throat and in my ears. I try not to pay attention to the frown on his face. Dr Roberts only frowns when something is wrong. Like the day he told me I had to go into hospital or I would die, or the day he told Lil the cancer had spread.

"Hmmm." The doctor unplugs his stethoscope from his ears.

"Not good, doc?" A resigned dread settles in the pit of my stomach.

"You've definitely got an infection brewing. Have you spent much time outdoors in the cold?"

I can't help the blush that spreads across my cheeks, and from his raised eyebrows I can see the doctor notices.

"Oh? Oh...." Dr Roberts sighs. "Well, stay indoors for anything like that. You aren't well enough for outdoor... activities in the freezing cold. I'll give you some antibiotics and you should be fine." He finishes his scolding and sits down next to me to write the prescription. As he signs his name, the doctor looks up with such a serious expression that the feeling of dread comes back again. "You've got to take care of yourself, Danny. I mean it. You can't afford to take any risks with your lungs. I've seen homeless kids dead within a week simply because they think they're invincible."

"David," I say firmly.

He looks confused.

"My name is David, not Danny. And I won't take any more risks."

Dr Roberts nods. "David. I'm sorry. You're a sensible lad. That's why you've survived this long."

I'm partly offended. He's not *that* much older than me, and I can't have the hots for someone who thinks I'm a boy. Still, he's a happily married man with two kids and dog. I need to put those adolescent fantasies aside and start thinking about the one who really wants me.

There's a soft knock at the door, and when we both say, "Come in," Ben pokes his head around the door.

"Hi," he says. "Liam needs to see you, Doc. His feet are bad again."

The doctor pulls a face. "Only if someone holds his legs. Last time he nearly broke my jaw when he kicked me."

"I'll do it," I say, getting to my feet. Better than looking at those prospectuses of kids with happy, shining faces a minute longer.

Ben gives me and then the books a knowing look. "You'd rather hold onto Liam's legs than look at extending your education?"

"They're"—I wave at the books—"not me."

"You can always study online," Dr Roberts suggests. "That way you could work maybe part time and study part time."

Ben and I nod at the same time. That sounds more like me. I don't think I could be surrounded by young kids all day, every day.

"Let's get this over and done with," the doctor mutters. "You do know how to ruin a man's day, Ben."

Maybe it was unprofessional, but the doctor has a point. Liam's a long-term homeless, virtually uncommunicative except with his fists. His feet and legs are ulcerated and in such a state he needs to be in hospital, but he refuses to go and when they do get him there, he leaves as soon as he can walk again.

I don't want to get like Liam, and I could see it happening. Whatever the outcome of my current situation, there has to be more for me than Liam's lot in life.

When I tell the ladies the results of the doctor's visit, Sylvia fusses and scolds over me until Mary tells her to leave me alone.

"The boy's all right. He just needs to take better care of himself. He's got something else to think about now."

I flush at the knowing look. "Can I do anything for you two? Shopping or housework? Otherwise I'm gonna kip before Jack turns up. My head hurts."

That sends Sylvia into more fussing. "You go to sleep. I'm not going to let you do anything until you're better."

Mary rolls her eyes at her daughter. "Don't be ridiculous, Sylv. He just needs the pills." She waves her hand at my door. "Go to sleep for a while, David. I'll wake you if we need anything. Do you need some painkillers?"

"I bought some when I got the antibiotics, thanks," I say.

Sylvia wants to tuck me in but Mary tells her to knock it off. Relieved, I scurry away before she follows through on her threat.

I take one of the antibiotics. It's huge and tastes foul but I swallow it down with plenty of water and chase it up with two paracetamol.

I go to sleep with my arms wrapped around the pillow Jack used last night. It smells of him and I inhale deeply, comforted by his smell.

I'm woken up by something.... I'm not sure what... and it makes me sit up with a start, my heart slamming in my chest.

"David, what's the matter?" Jack looks up at me with concern, blinking sleepily.

I lie back down and clutch on to him. "I... how long have you been there?" I ask.

"About half an hour. Sylvia told me you weren't feeling good, so I thought we could relax rather than go out tonight." Jack holds me tightly, enveloping me in his arms. I press myself against him, not sure what has made me so frightened.

"We don't have to do that. Let's go to the pub."

I need to get out from here. Think of something else."

"Are you sure? I'm happy to watch TV."

I shake my head. "It's only a chest infection. I've got antibiotics and it's not catching."

He looks at me dubiously. "If you're sure."

"I'm sure."

I've got to get away from the noise in my head, and the pub seems as good a place as any—no alcohol though.

"The local club is having a gay night. Normally it's over twenty-ones, but they've reduced it to eighteens and over as long as you have ID. Do you want to go?"

My eyes widen. I've never been to a club. It might be just what I need to take me out of myself. "I don't have any ID."

"What?" Jack looks puzzled.

"No ID."

"Not a passport or a driver's license or something?"

I shake my head. "Nothing."

Jacks looks momentarily disappointed and then he shrugs. "Oh well. We'll just go to the pub." At my look of horror, he says, "No snakebite, I promise. We'll stick to Coke this time. Do you want to tell Mary you're going?"

"Not if Sylvia's there. She won't let me out of the house."

He grins. "Was she fussing?"

I shudder. "You have no idea. She was worse than my...." I stop. I was going to mention my mother but she has no place here.

Jack arches an eyebrow. "Than your…?"

"Doesn't matter," I mutter. "Have I got time to take a shower?"

"It's only half seven. Plenty of time."

I head for the shower, stripping off as I go. I turn the water on. As I straighten, a very warm and very naked body plasters itself against me.

"Thought I'd join you in case you needed someone to wash your back."

I shiver under the rush of water. The feel of his dick and his warm breath in my ear is a real turn-on, and my cock responds accordingly.

"You can wash me." My voice is squeaky with need.

Jack laughs—the bastard—and then he's soaping my back, and my arse, and other parts of me, and I forget to be embarrassed about my voice.

"Fuck," I breathe out as he slides his hand up my dick.

"Is that what you want?" Jack asks. "Want me to fuck you against the wall?"

The way I press my arse into him is answer enough. I'm cold momentarily, while he gets the lube, and then he's back, pressing a slick finger into my arse. He's still new enough to this to take it slowly, not sure enough of my body or his skill to rush preparing me. I appreciate the care he's taking, too used to being taken without any thought of my needs.

"Is this okay?" he asks as he pushes in a third finger.

It's okay—it's more than okay—to have his

body against mine and his fingertips brushing my prostate. My hands clench involuntarily into fists from the sensation.

"Jesus, Jack!" I yell as the need to climax becomes more urgent.

Jack grunts as he enters me. Even with the care he's taken, I have to take a deep breath as my body resists, then he's filling me up with his cock, his body hard against mine.

Jack drops his head to my shoulder and he takes deep breaths as he tries to gain some control. "Fuck, if I move I'm going to blow," he mutters into my ear.

"Isn't that the point?" I ask, grinning at him, and then I end up coughing at water going in my mouth and the tightness in my chest.

"Jeez, don't do that," Jack groans.

It takes me a couple of minutes to stop coughing. "Do what? Choke?"

"Every time you cough it clamps on my dick. I feel like I've lost all the blood supply."

"Bet you don't feel like you're coming anymore," I point out.

He's quiet for a minute. "Bastard," he hisses.

"Uh-huh. Glad to be of service."

"You just stand there and let me fuck you."

I let him do what he wants to do.

Chapter 16

December 31

I shut the door firmly in the face of Mary's concern. She wants me to join her for the New Year celebration, but all I want to do is hide, as I have for the past three years. This time at least, I have a bed, rather than a hollow under a bush. Thankfully, Sylvia is working, because she would have made a fuss. Mary just kissed me on the cheek and went back to her sitting room with her sherry and the BBC.

I used to listen to the sounds of people celebrating, the drunken rowdiness as they walked through the park, and, occasionally, the heated gasps of lovers as they fucked against a tree or over the bench. I would clap my hands over my ears to avoid the sound of midnight and the cheers and fireworks.

This year, I climb into bed and cover my ears with headphones. I play Nickelback and hope I fall asleep. I want it to be light when I wake up, and for midnight to be a distant memory.

Jack is with his family. He tried to persuade me to join him but I was adamant, and he left me with a kiss and a promise of what he's going to do to me on New Year's Day. In my cocoon under the duvet, my cheeks heat. For a boy with no experience, he's learning fast. I'm wondering if the Internet has something to do with that.

I have to emerge from my cocoon when I get overheated. I roll over onto my back and close my eyes as I listen to the music. I can't believe I'm here, tucked up in a warm bed, rather than the hollow of my bush in the park. I can't believe I've done the one thing I promised myself I'd never do again: become dependent on other people. From the moment I agreed to go home with Sylvia, I've felt like a spinning top, totally out of control. I tell myself I had a choice, and I made the choice to move on, but I'm not sure that's true. Perhaps the only choice I had was whether to live or die. Facing death as a teenager was not an easy decision. My lungs would never have survived, though. I rub my chest, in more pain than I've been prepared to admit. Sylvia would have had me back in hospital if I'd opened my mouth.

I can't ignore it any longer. Sighing, I take off the headphones, get out of bed, and head towards the bathroom. I'm rooting through the cabinet for paracetamol when I hear the muffled sound of Big Ben striking the first chime from Mary's sitting room. I know that sound. It haunts every nightmare I've had for the past four years. I slam my hands over my ears to block it out, but it penetrates my head, chiming over and over again.

"Danny... Danny... shhh, you're safe. You're all right now. Come on, honey." Hands try to drag my hands away from my ears.

"No, no. Leave me alone." I bat the hands away

before they hurt me, begging them not to hurt me, *please, please don't hurt me again. I'll be good, don't throw me out.* Over and over I beg, wrapping my arms around my knees and rocking, backward and forward, but the chiming keeps on, keeps fucking on.

"Danny, stop it. You're safe now. I won't hurt you. I won't throw you out."

In the screaming funk in my head, a firm voice tells me to calm down. I don't understand what it means, but it keeps talking. Eventually, I understand the voice is Mary's. I open my eyes, blinking in confusion as I realise we're both on the bathroom floor.

"What happened?" I ask, my voice a croaky mess.

The relief on Mary's face is obvious. "I heard you screaming. I came in to find you here, screaming your head off." She gets to her feet and holds out a hand. "Come on, let's get you back to bed, and you can tell me what set you off."

Ignoring her hand, I get up, swaying from the rush in my head.

"For heaven's sake...," she mutters and slides an arm around my waist. Mary doesn't let go until I'm beside the bed. "Get in," she says. "I'll make us a drink."

I lie down and close my eyes, wanting to block her out, and her concern. It's weighing me down. I keep them closed until the bed dips as Mary sits down next to me.

"Shall we start with what just happened there?" she asks.

"Nothing." I turn my head away from her.

"Danny, you seem to be under the misapprehension that I'm stupid."

I turn to look at her then. "I don't think you're stupid."

She looks at me steadily. "Then tell me why I found you screaming on my bathroom floor."

I swallow several times, unable to say the words that will make me look like the idiot I am. But she waits patiently, her intent gaze telling me better than words that I can't avoid the subject. "I heard the chimes of Big Ben from the TV. I panicked."

Mary nods. "Has this happened before?"

"Once. I was on my own, though. Nobody saw. I woke up to a black eye I gave myself."

She reaches over to hold my hand. "I think you need to see a doctor."

"I'm not hurt this time." Apart from my chest, which feels so tight.

"I mean a psychiatrist."

I try to pull my hand away, but she hangs on to it. "A shrink?"

"You are obviously traumatised by what happened. They might be able to make sense of it for you."

I tug my hand away then and wrap my arms around my knees. "What is there to make sense of? My dad threw me out at New Year. I have issues about Big fucking Ben."

"Don't swear," Mary says, but there's no heat in her words. She looks worried. It makes me worried.

I want to shout and scream at her, but I'm not a

fucking kid anymore.

"Here." She hands me a hot chocolate.

I don't need the drink, but she'll only fuss if I don't take it. I sip it cautiously. "What's in this?" I ask.

"Whiskey," Mary says. "You need to sleep rather than lie here fretting."

"Sylvia wouldn't approve."

"Sylvia doesn't need to know," she snaps.

It tastes odd, but I deal. I'm tired, and the thought of sleeping appeals. "I'm sorry for frightening you."

She waves her hand. "It takes more than an odd scream to frighten me."

"I guess you've seen it all before."

"I've seen many kids who refuse to admit anything's wrong," she says. "They're the ones who run away."

"I've survived this long by myself."

"And now you don't have to." Mary looks at me kindly. "Don't fight the help, Danny. You need it."

"David."

Mary nods. "David. I'm sorry, I forgot."

I lie back against the pillows and close my eyes. Mary strokes my forehead and then she leaves me alone with a whispered, "Happy New Year, David."

I can't bring myself to whisper it back.

January 1, 2004

Jack drags me down to the river. He's all excited and bouncy, and I've no idea what the fuck for. One thing I do notice is he's wearing glasses, rather than his blue contact lenses, and his green eyes have dark shadows under them.

"Heavy night last night?" I ask.

I see the look of guilt on his face and the puppy-like bouncing stops.

"Jack?"

"I don't want you to be angry," he says immediately.

I shrug. "Okay." I bury my hands in the pockets of my coat because it's fucking freezing.

He looks surprised. "Just like that? You're not angry?"

"Do I have something to be angry about?"

Jack sighs and turns to look at the river. "Two of my school friends came over last night. We got drunk."

"I didn't know you had any friends at school." Actually, that isn't true. I remember Harry talking about a couple of friends.

"Thanks," he says, looking offended. "I had one or two."

"I'm sorry. You just said you were lonely."

He nods. "They weren't close friends, but we had classes together. Our parents were friends."

"Did you have a good time?" I ask, trying to make things better. The last thing I want to do is make Jack angry or upset.

"Yeah," he nodded. "I wish you'd been there, though. I wanted to introduce them to my boyfriend. I don't think they believe you exist."

"Why the fuck not?"

"They never met Danny, although I talked

about him all the time."

"Jack, have you seen you? You're hot. You should have boys queuing around the block."

He beams at me. "I only want one boy."

"So why have you dragged me down here?"

Jack starts ticking off his fingers. "One, you need the fresh air. Two, I need the fresh air. Three, you need to get away from Mary and Sylvia sometimes. Four, this is the first place we went to...." He pauses.

I arch one eyebrow. "And five?"

"How do you know there is a five?"

"You're telling me there isn't?"

He grins and bounces again. "You know me too well. Okay, five, I'm coming to live in England for good. I'll have to wait until I graduate high school but then I'm coming to college over here. Isn't that great?"

I stare at Jack in horror. "No. No, you can't do that."

He frowns. "But I've arranged it. Well, I will do as soon as I get home. Don't you want me to stay here?"

"No." I walk away as quickly as I can, furious at him out of all proportion.

"David, wait up, what's wrong? I thought you'd love it if we stayed together?"

I can hear the hurt in Jack's voice but.... I stop suddenly, turning to face him. "You can't just change your whole life on the basis of one fling."

Jack stares at me with huge eyes. "Fling? Is that all I am to you? I thought you loved me."

I shake my head. "It's too much, Jack. You don't

know me. You think I can deal with this? No, no, no."

"David...."

"Leave me alone." I walk off as fast as I can, desperate to get away.

Why don't these people understand? They're stripping away every layer of independence I have. I've got nothing left. Nothing of me, and nothing of Danny/David—whoever the fuck I am.

I can't go back to the flat. Briefly I contemplate going to the park, but my chest hurts too much. Instead, I go to the one other place I feel safe.

Ben looks up as I walk in through the shabby door. "Hey, David." He seems about to say something else, and then he catches sight of my face.

"Need to talk?"

I nod tightly, holding myself together with an effort.

Ben looks over to one of the girls behind the counter. "Kisa, take over here, will you?"

Kisa nods, looking at me curiously. I don't recognise her.

Ben leads me into the office and offers me the armchair. I sit down on the edge. Ben sits on the office chair and looks at me expectantly.

"I can't do this," I burst out.

"Do what?" he asks.

"This. All of it."

"David, take a deep breath and start at the beginning. What's happened?"

"I...." Ben waits patiently as I try to collect my thoughts. "Jack wants to transfer over here to a local university. Mary wants me to see a psychiatrist. You want me to start school."

Understanding dawns in Ben's face.

"You feel trapped?" he asks.

"You have no idea how I feel," I yell. "Everyone's making decisions for me except me."

"No one can force you to do anything," Ben says gently.

"It doesn't feel like it." I wrap my arms around myself, feeling like I'm going to fly apart at any moment. "I was free in the park."

"David, I know how you feel. You know I do."

I stare at him blankly. "I need to get away."

"Running away isn't going to help. You need to talk to people, and you're going to have to listen to people as well."

"No one is listening to me."

"Yes, they are, David. You're just not talking. All you do is burst out when they suggest something."

I laugh sharply. "Jack wasn't *suggesting*."

"Jack's eighteen. He's still a kid and overenthusiastic. He's thinking with his dick."

It's the last thing I expect to hear coming out of sweet and gentle Ben's mouth, and I say so.

Ben shrugs. "I remember that age. I'd just discovered what it was for, and I was determined to use it."

"It doesn't help that I'm being hassled on all sides. I need a break, Ben. They all tell me what to do, what to wear, when to fuck. I can't breathe." And then I really *can't* breathe, and I'm clutching my chest in pain.

Ben's at my side immediately, rubbing my

back in small circles. "Okay, you just calm down, David. I'm going to handle this with you."

There's a knock at the door and Kisa pokes her head around. "Ben, Mary's on the phone, looking for David."

Ben looked up. "Tell her David's fine, and he'll be home later. He's just giving me a hand with the new cupboards."

"You don't look so good, David," Kisa says. "Panic attack?"

"That, and a chest infection," Ben agrees.

"Okay, I'll tell her." She nods and closes the door.

"She's a good worker," Ben says.

I slump against the back of the chair. A short attack this time. I should be relieved.

"I think you need to see the doctor again," Ben says, moving back to his chair. "I can hear your chest rattling from here."

"They said if I got pneumonia again, it would kill me."

"You've had two months in the dry and warm, and spent most of it asleep. You're not in the same position you were in last time you were taken into hospital. Let me call Doc Roberts."

I shake my head, not wanting to disturb the poor man. "It's New Year's Day. Let him have the day off."

"He's on call for the shelter," Ben says as he reaches for the phone.

"I'm not one of the clients anymore."

Ben looks at me seriously. "Yes, you are. Until you're settled at Mary's house, you are one of my clients."

"I am settled," I protest.

"No, you aren't. If you were, you wouldn't be having a panic attack and running back here."

"I'm fine," I say, and then I spoil it by coughing so hard I end up doubled over, holding my stomach as I retch.

Ben waits until the coughing fit subsides, then hands me a drink of water and calls the doctor. The conversation is short and sweet, and within twenty minutes, Dr Roberts is listening to my chest for the second time in three days.

He frowns as he takes his stethoscope out of his ears. "You need a chest X-ray," he says. "Did the antibiotics help at all?"

"I don't think they've had a chance to," I say.

"You need to have your sputum tested and have a chest X-ray. With your history, we need to get you back to hospital."

"I'm fine!" I stand up, ignoring the fact I feel like shit.

Ben presses me back into the chair. "This is not telling you what to do. This is saving your life. David, you can walk out that door, but there's a chance you'll die without proper medical attention. Everything else can wait. Jack, the psychiatrist, Mary and Sylvia. All of them can wait. Go to the hospital and get checked out."

Dr Roberts keeps quiet while Ben gives his speech. When Ben falls silent, the doctor looks at me. "You coming?"

I nod. What else can I do?

As we leave the building, Jack rushes up to the

door. His brown hair is plastered to his red and sweaty face.

"David, where are you going? Talk to me?"

Ben deliberately steps between me and Jack. "David needs to go to the hospital to get his chest checked out."

"I'll come with you," Jack says immediately, trying to step around Ben.

Ben opens his mouth to speak, but I hold up my hand. "Not now, Jack. You don't need to spend the day looking after me. Go home. I'll call you when I get back to Mary's."

Jack steps forward and grabs hold of me, screwing up his face with worry. "I want to come with you. I made you run off."

I lean forward and kiss him, a gentle brush of lips. His mouth clings to mine. "It's not your fault. I was being an idiot. Let me get this X-ray over and done with and we can talk." I don't tell him I might end up being admitted again. He doesn't need to know that. I'm starting to realise there are limitations to my love. I can't take on his issues as well as my own.

He steps back. "If you don't call, I'm coming to the hospital," he warns.

I bite my lip. I might have limitations, but this boy is going to bulldoze through them all.

"Jack, let's get David sorted, and I promise one of us will call you," Ben says.

It's obvious he's reluctant to let me go, but he steps back as Ben guides me to the car.

"Call me," he mouths as we drive away.

The hospital keeps me in—surprise, surprise. Bronchitis and pneumonia. I'm hooked up to an IV and told to sit, stay. Woof!

To be honest, I'm so tired and emotionally knackered by the time I get through A&E and into a bed, I don't have the energy to do anything else except sleep. I don't even have the strength to be worried about the death sentence the doctors laid upon me last time.

I can't say I'm particularly surprised to see Jack sitting beside the bed when I wake up. He's reading a book and doesn't notice immediately I'm awake.

"Hey." My mouth is dry and it comes out as more of a croak, but Jack looks up, a smile across his face.

"Hi. You're awake."

"I'll get back to you on that. How long have you been here?"

"Half an hour."

I roll over, wincing as the stent pulls in my hand, and look outside. It's already dark. "What's the time?"

"About six."

"Shouldn't you be at your grandmother's?"

"Yep." He sounds odd and he looks away.

I sigh. "You in trouble?"

"Yeah. Grandma is annoyed with me."

"You should be there," I say as gently as I can. I don't want him to get into trouble with his family because of me, and I don't want to fight with him.

Jack pulls up a chair to the bed and reaches out

to hold my hand. His skin looks very tan against mine. "I know this scares you, but you are more important. You are my lover, and we are going to be together forever."

"You're eighteen and just a kid. You can't say things like that."

He looks fierce as he holds on to me even tighter. It hurts, but I don't want him to let go of me. "What do you want me to say? I feel like I've known you forever rather than just a week."

"You don't know me." It sounds weak and pathetic even to me.

"And whose fault is that? You're so fucking full of secrets, David."

"I'm...."

He glares at me so fiercely I shut up. "You're going to lie there, and get better, and I'm going to sit with you, and we *will* be together. Do you understand?"

I look into his tired eyes, and suddenly I realise this boy is determined to keep me. Me. Loser. Hooker. Jack or Harry, he doesn't care who I am. He just wants me. I don't believe it will last. I don't have that naïve innocence he does.

Jack leans forward, holding my wrist tight. "I lost my mum. I'm not going to lose you."

And then maybe he isn't so innocent after all. He has lost, and now he knows what he wants. Jack wants me. Why am I putting up such a fight? I have a home, I have a family of sorts, and I have Jack.

I yawn suddenly and his face softens. "Go back to sleep, David. I'll read for a bit and go home for dinner. Then I'll be back this evening."

"You should see your friends."

Jack shakes his head. "I've seen them. Tonight I'm spending with you."

I close my eyes, aware he's still holding my wrist. Jack's lying, of course. He has no intention of going home. He'll be there when I wake up. He's a Klingon.

"A Klingon? You think I'm a Klingon?" Jack sounds really offended.

I open one eye. "Did I say that out loud?"

He nods, and then he shrugs. "I don't mind being your Klingon."

"Do I get a choice?"

Jack brushes my ear with his lips. "No. After all, I am yours... sir."

A smile curves my lips. Jack is mine. I like that idea.

Epilogue

August 2012

I wait.

The silence is overwhelming in the tiny room. I don't dare look at his face—haven't, in fact, since I started my story. Jack hasn't said a word, hasn't tried to interrupt. Not even a gasp at some of the less savoury parts.

Jack speaks eventually. "You knew it was me."

"Yes."

"All this time you knew I was Harry."

"Yes."

"And you never told me that the boy in the park—*my first love*—was you." The words come out on a breathy gasp, and I can tell he's fighting back tears.

"No."

"Would you have ever told me?"

I sigh, and decide to be honest, even if it means losing Jack for good. "Probably not. No."

"Why not?"

"Because I never want to remember what it was like to be that boy."

"Even if it means forgetting me?"

I look up then, making sure he can hear the

sincerity in my voice. "I will *never* forget you, *never.* You were the only shining moment in three years of misery."

"But not enough to tell me the boy who looked after me for so long, who gave me my first blow job, the one I treasured in my heart as my first, the one I *told* you about...." Jack runs out of breath before he can finish the sentence. Or maybe he just runs out of strength.

I reach out a hand to hold his, trying not to show how hurt I am when he flinches away. "Jack, please...."

"Please what?" he roars, getting to his feet. Then he's leaning over me, anger radiating from every pore.

It's my turn to flinch. I've never been scared of Jack, even though he's much bigger than me. The willowy youth has been replaced with a man of solid muscle, born of many hours at the gym. But after the hours of talking about my past, I'm vulnerable and he's too big as he looms over me.

"You think I'm going to hurt you? Me? I've never even... God!" He runs his hand through his hair, leaving it sticking up in all directions. "I would never lay a finger on you, David, you must know that?"

"I do," I admit quietly. Jack's the gentlest man alive, and he would never hurt me physically.

"Then why did you flinch away from me?"

"I don't know. I thought... just... you were so angry. I was scared."

His face crumples at my words, and Jack falls on his knees in front of me, burying his face in my lap. I stroke his head, smoothing his hair from where he'd ruffled it before, murmuring soothing noises as he shakes with pent-up emotion.

"I thought I'd never see you again. I just wanted to say thank you for everything you'd done for me. It all happened so fast."

"It wasn't your fault." Hell, I don't blame him for disappearing. The poor guy lost his mother in a car accident and then was shipped off to America by a father who didn't know which end was up. Jack's father is a good man, but his handle on his son's psyche is tenuous at best.

Jack raises his head, his large green eyes filled with tears. "Why didn't you tell me it was you?"

"I thought you'd recognise me, and when you didn't, I thought maybe it was for the best. Why would you want anything to do with a bum like Danny? In the beginning, I was going to tell you and then it got harder and harder to be honest with you. And we'd been together for so long I thought you'd forget about Danny and just concentrate on me."

Jack sniffles and hiccups. "You think I'd forget about the boy who protected me and showed me it was okay to be queer?"

I brush his bottom lip with the pad of my thumb. "I was no one."

"You were the only one," he corrects. He leans forward and kisses me. "I've spent my life regretting I never got a chance to say good-bye to Danny."

I give him a wan smile. "Danny doesn't exist anymore."

Jack sits back on his haunches. "Yes, he does. You think you left him behind when you became David Miles? Don't you realise all your actions are affected by that time?"

I frown at him. "What do you mean?"

"Look at the way you volunteer at the homeless shelter. I thought you were just a great guy. I didn't realise it was personal. What about the way you obsessively make this place a home, or the fact you refuse to have joint bank accounts in case we split up and 'we need to be financially independent.' You never celebrate New Year, and when was the last time you stepped into that park?"

All of it is true. Kinda. I still can't hear Big Ben's chimes without the cold icy fear of what could happen next. Having separate bank accounts just makes sense, and as for volunteering, well, Jack did that too. That's how we met. I say as much, and am taken aback by the smile that spreads across his face.

"Of course I did, you idiot. As soon as we flew back, I made the family volunteer at the shelter. I was praying I'd see Danny, only no one would tell me what happened other than he was 'dead'. I thought my world had come to an end, and then I met you." He tilts his head, a knowing look in his eyes. "Did they know it was you?"

"One or two of the staff at the shelter," I admit. "Sylvia and Ben. Greg, as well. But they would never have betrayed my confidence. They thought I was an idiot getting involved with you."

"Sylvia and Ben?" I hear the hurt still in his

voice and I understand it. Sylvia and Ben are two of our closest friends. Now he finds out they've been keeping secrets.

"They are the only two. And Doc Roberts. I have no other past friends. Ben is one of Mary's kids. They would never have told you anything I didn't want you to hear. We protect our own."

Jack draws in a shaky breath. It's a lot for him to take in, and I don't try to comfort him again. He's got to process this by himself. I just hope our relationship is strong enough to survive the fact I've been lying to him all this time.

"You love me. Is that real?" he demands.

"Yes."

"And you aren't about to walk out or do anything as stupid as that?"

"Not going anywhere," I assure him.

"Who are you really, David?"

"David Miles."

Jack shakes his head. "Not the name you have now, or when you met me. The name you were born with. What is your real name?"

"Martin Daniel Gibson." God, I haven't heard that name for so long. Martin Daniel Gibson, son of Martin Peter Gibson and Maureen Catherine Gibson. They'd called me Danny from the time I was born to distinguish me from my dad.

"You changed your name."

"New start, new life."

"Why David Miles?"

I liked Miles. The road travelled and the journey to come. David was an exceptionally good fuck I met once in the park. "I just liked the name." I'm not *that* stupid.

He fixes me with a direct stare. "How many more secrets am I going to find out?"

I chew on the inside of my mouth. I could lie, but it'll come back to bite me on the arse—look at this evening. "I have secrets. I'm not going to tell you everything that happened to me in those three years. You don't need to know that. I didn't tell Harry, and I won't tell you."

"Why not?" he demands. "You're my partner. I should know those things to share your pain."

I hold back the derisive snort. Pop Psychology 101. "Do you think knowing about the worst times in my life will help us as a couple?" I ask as gently as I can.

Jack wriggles under my gaze and then sighs. "No. I just can't bear the thought of you dealing with it all alone."

"I'm not alone. I have you, and that's all I need. Martin Daniel Gibson is as dead as Danny now, as Harry is to you. I have a life with you, a roof over my head, and I'm happy. That's all I need."

And finally, finally, I see Jack relax, and I let out the breath I've been holding.

Jack gets to his feet and holds out his hand. "Come to bed with me?"

"Like I'd ever say no?" I'd never refuse to love my Jack. I place my hand in his and let him take me into the bedroom.

Jack undresses me with shaking hands and murmured endearments. I let him take the lead this time, knowing he needs to reconnect with David, but also that he's saying hello and good-bye to Danny, his first love.

I don't mind. In my head, I say good-bye to Danny too. Maybe being that frightened kid on the streets, the kid who traded blow jobs for burgers and a chance to have a wash, is still me. I can't get away from my past no matter how hard I try. But it didn't destroy me, and the man who kneels at my feet is proof of that.

One evening, I'll take Jack into the park and we'll lie in the short grass and relive our past love. Or maybe not. Maybe I'll let sleeping dogs lie and the ghosts of two boys blow away in the wind.

Also by Sue Brown

STANDALONE books

Summer's Dawn | Summer's Song | A Tale Told in Darkness | A Cock in the Window | In-Decision | The Backpack | The Clumsy Santa | Mr Plum | Chance to Be King | Made for Aaron | Gabriel's Storm

Final Admission | The Layered Mask | The Next Call | The Night Porter | Light of Day | The Sky Is Dead | Nothing Ever Happens | Stolen Dreams | Waiting | Prey Time | Louis Hates Valentines Day | Racing Raindrops | The Fireman's Pole | Falling for Ramos | Last Place in the Chalet | Snow Twink | Winter Prince

JT'S BAR series

Alpha Barman | Alpha Chef | Alpha Home | Alpha Valentine | Alpha Protect | Alpha Hunt | Alpha Rush

BIKER DADDY BODYGUARDS series

Hold Firm | Hold Close | Hold Safe | Hold Firm

ANGEL ENTERPRISES series

Morning My Angel | Goodnight My Angel | Hello

My Angel

LYON ROAD VETS series
Hairy Harry's Car Seat | Bob, the Destroyer of Leads | Hazel Takes Over | Stormin' Norman | Lyon Road Vets Boxset

COWBOYS AND ANGELS series
Speed Dating the Boss | Secretly Dating the Lionman | Slow Dating the Detective

WITH A KICK series (with Clare London)
Hissed as a Newt | Bells and Balls

FRANKIE'S series
Frankie & Al | Ed & Marchant | Anthony & Leo | Jordan & Rhys |

THE ISLE series
The Isle of... Where? | Isle of Wishes | Isle of Waves | Isle of Waiting | Island Doctor | Island Counsellor

MORNING REPORT series

Morning Report | Complete Faith | Go-to Guy |
Luke's Present | Letters From a Cowboy |

About Sue Brown

Cranky middle-aged author with an addiction for coffee, and a passion for romancing two guys. She loves her dog, she loves her kids, and she loves coffee; in which order very much depends on the time of day.

Come over and talk to Sue at:
Newsletter:
https://landing.mailerlite.com/webforms/landing/zlh7c3
Bookbub: https://www.bookbub.com/profile/sue-brown
Patreon:
https://www.patreon.com/suebrownstories
Website: http://www.suebrownstories.com/
Facebook group:
https://www.facebook.com/SueBrownsStories/
Twitter: http://twitter.com/suebrownstories
Email: sue@suebrownstories.com

www.ingramcontent.com/pod-product-compliance
Lightning Source LLC
Chambersburg PA
CBHW021949120726
47992CB00001B/219